Trapped!, an incredible story of survival, is based on a true incident. . . .

TRAPPED!

Arthur Roth

SCHOLASTIC INC.
New York Toronto London Auckland Sydney

To John Vihtelic,
who lived it all
and more

ISBN 0-590-32629-5

 Published by Scholastic Inc.

12 11 10 9 1 2 3 4/9

Printed in the U.S.A. 01

The car sailed out into space, then tumbled end over end. It struck a ledge ten feet down with a force that knocked the breath from Jimmy. He heard the awful, rending crash of torn metal and was thrown across the front seat. A numbing pain tore through his right arm as it struck the partially opened vent window on the passenger's side. The wagon continued its slow-motion fall, bouncing off the ledge, turning turtle, and sliding down the cliff upside down. . . .

Chapter One

Jimmy Korne hit the brakes the moment he spotted the deer in the headlights. The animal rose from the bushes and seemed to float over the hood and roof of his car. The station wagon's front wheels skidded in the loose gravel on the edge of the road. Jimmy spun the steering wheel and tried to straighten the locking wheels, afraid of the steep ravine he knew he was headed for.

The nose of the car dipped as it went off the shoulder, and Jimmy instinctively grabbed the steering wheel with both hands, braced his arms, and pressed back against the seat. He was going to crash!

The car sailed out into space, then tumbled end over end. It struck a ledge ten feet down with a force that knocked the breath from Jimmy. He heard the awful, rending crash of torn metal and was thrown across the front seat. A numbing pain tore through his right arm as it struck the partially opened vent window on the passenger's side. The wagon continued its slow-motion fall, bouncing off the ledge, turning turtle, and sliding down the cliff face upside down.

Jimmy was briefly aware of being upside down. He felt his forehead pressing against a door armrest and tried to grab something to steady himself. The screech of rock scraping metal assaulted his ears, and he could feel the car strike a tree, snapping off branches with cracks like rifle shots. Then the car flipped outward from a ledge and landed upright on the floor of the ravine with a final, jarring wallop that shook every bone in Jimmy's body.

Still dazed from the impact, Jimmy's bewildered mind replayed the initial scene of the crash. He was to go over that scene hundreds of times in the next couple of weeks. What always surprised him was how long the action seemed to take: the dramatic appearance of the deer as the headlights picked the animal out cleanly against the dark brush and trees of the forest; that slow, arching leap as the deer seemingly took wing and floated over the onrushing car; the delicate beauty of the four legs tucked up into the white fur of the animal's belly; the thudding crack of hooves on the road as the deer landed. The whole scene couldn't have lasted more than two or three seconds, yet it seemed to unroll at its own slow-motion speed that had nothing to do with real time. And through all of this he had been aware of the car's relentless skid toward the edge of the ravine.

Pain forced Jimmy out of his daze. He was

alive and suddenly very aware of everything around him: a single headlamp flooding the undergrowth with light through which a cloud of dust, smoke, and steam was rising; the sound of the engine still running; the harsh stench of gasoline from a broken fuel tank. He was aware, too, that the wagon had landed right side up. Suddenly the full horror of his situation hit home. One spark and the car would go up in a ball of roaring flame! He had to turn off the engine.

Jimmy stared into the darkness, trying to find the ignition and the key. The whole front seat had broken, folded down almost flat, and he was lying back on the passenger's side, looking up at the dented roof of the car. He tried to sit up, but the ceiling was too low. Then he tried to wiggle out, but his right foot was caught in something, and he couldn't get it loose. He had to reach those car keys! He squirmed, and the fingertips of his left hand were just able to reach the key ring dangling from the ignition. The key itself was covered with some sort of fluid that made it slippery, but he caught the rounded end and cautiously turned it. The engine stuttered into silence. In the reflected glow that came from the still-lit headlamp, he saw that the fluid on the key was blood.

At the same time he tasted blood in his mouth, and a bolt of fear shot through him. Had he ruptured something? He held his breath as though listening to the inner workings of his body. Fluid pooled in the corner of his mouth and he realized, with some relief, that the blood was from a cut somewhere on his head and was not an internal injury.

Jimmy knew he wasn't out of danger yet. That headlight was still on, and a short circuit of any kind could still send the car up in a sheet of flame. The light switch was a rocker button on the extreme left edge of the instrument panel, beyond his reach.

He felt around on the floor, hoping to find something long enough to reach the button and press it down. After patting around, his left hand found a piece of wood that felt like a broomstick. It was a plumber's helper, a two-foot-long wooden handle with a rubber cup at one end. His father had borrowed it from a friend, then thrown it in the car to return the next time he stopped by his house. After several moments of fumbling around, Jimmy was able to place the rounded end of the handle against the rocker switch. It slipped off three times before he finally managed to press the button. The headlight went out, plunging his world into darkness. There — at least he wouldn't be burned alive.

Through all of his actions, Jimmy had been aware of a rushing noise in the background, as though a strong wind were blowing through the treetops. But now he listened more carefully and decided the car had wound up on the bank of a mountain stream. In fact, the car had tumbled clear over the creek before it came to rest. At the moment, though, the value of having water nearby didn't dawn on him. Jimmy had more important things to worry about — his injuries.

He had that cut on his head, probably caused by a piece of flying glass. Except for one corner, the whole windshield had shattered and broken. The side windows, too, were missing most of their glass. He reached up to his forehead and felt the cut. It was still bleeding, but the wound didn't seem deep, and he guessed it was no more than an inch long. A far greater worry was his right arm. That sleeve was soaked with blood. He tried to sit up, but the partially collapsed ceiling gave too little headway. Somehow, he had to fix that arm, stop the bleeding. He managed to roll up the shirt-sleeve. With his eyes now accustomed to the dark, he was able to see the wound.

The cut, just below the elbow, was deep and jagged and at least six inches long. As he probed through the blood and torn flesh, he felt tiny bits of glass. Gritting his teeth against the pain, he picked out as many slivers of glass as he could feel. He wondered whether he could bleed to death. He should stop the bleeding, that much he knew. Jimmy had taken a first aid course in school, and he tried to remember now what the teacher had told them. It was something about pressure points and veins and arteries. Cut arteries spurted blood, while veins bled slowly. He should find the nearest pressure point between the wound and the heart and press on it until the bleeding stopped. A tourniquet could be used, but finger pressure was much safer. Anyway, his cut was bleeding slowly, which meant a vein and not an artery, and that wasn't as serious.

Jimmy straightened his right arm and pressed three fingers of his left hand on his elbow. He made himself count to one hundred. The bleeding seemed to stop, or at least slow down. He went back to pressing on the pressure point, this time for about five minutes. When he lifted his hand, there was no sign of further bleeding. He knew he should now put a tight bandage on the wound.

Jimmy dug his Swiss army knife out of his pocket and sawed the left sleeve off his shirt. He tied it around his right arm, making a rough bandage. Then he rolled his right sleeve down all the way to keep dirt out of his wound.

He felt a sense of gratification and surprise. He had done everything left-handed, with one leg trapped under the dashboard. Now he said aloud the first words he had uttered since the crash: "Not bad for a klutz, eh, Dad?"

His father — who could do anything with his hands, from sewing a hem on a curtain to building an entire house — had a low opinion of his elder son's ability to handle tools. He often called Jimmy the "Great Klutz." Though Jimmy always laughed when his father said that, inwardly he boiled with an anger his dad never suspected. His father didn't mean to be cruel, Jimmy knew. It was just an old family nickname that only his father kept using.

Jimmy lay back on the seat, prepared to wait out the long hours of the night. Surely someone would find him in the morning. They would notice the skid marks, then look over the edge, and see his car down in the bottom of the ravine. All he had to do was hang in there. In the morning he would blow the horn at the first car he heard passing by.

He spent a few more minutes trying to free his right leg, but no matter how he twisted or turned his foot, it remained caught. He gave up. He would work on it in the morning, when he could see better. Anyway, he shouldn't put any strain on his right arm now. It would only start bleeding again. He tried to relax and listen for cars on the road above. His own car's motor was giving off occasional, light clicks as it cooled down. Now he could hear the stream plainly and wondered how he could have mistaken it for the wind.

Soon he felt chilly and struggled into his denim jacket. A sleeping bag was somewhere in the car, too. Jimmy groped around with his left hand and came up with the plumber's helper again, and then a six-inch section that had broken off a carpenter's folding rule. He dropped them with disgust. At last his hand reached something soft.

He pulled the sleeping bag forward, spread it over himself, and tried to sleep. *Some graduation night*, he thought. If anyone had told him it would end like this, he would have said that person was crazy.

Now, with every movement of his arms and

legs, he began to feel new aches and bruises from the beating his body had taken. It was so unfair. First the news about Charlene, and now this. Why all the bad luck? However, he was alive, never mind the cuts and bruises. But he felt scared and very lonely, even though it wasn't the first night he had spent all alone in the woods.

Then it struck him — maybe he wasn't alone. Maybe people were camping nearby or something. He started shouting for help. "Hey! Anybody out there?"

He felt foolish but kept on calling. "Help! I'm trapped! Help! Please help! Is anybody out there? Help! Help!" A moment's silence; then he whispered, "Charlene?"

But the rushing murmur of stream water was the only sound that came back to him out of the night and the darkness.

He bunched up the sleeping bag and laid his head on it.

Chapter Two

Jimmy slept in brief snatches through the night. Once he thought he heard a car, but when he struggled around and looked up at the road, he saw nothing. As dawn broke and light filtered through the trees, he half sat up and stared out the windshield. A brown bird was drinking at the edge of the stream. It would dip its beak, then throw its head back to let the water ease down its throat. The bird turned and hopped up the bank, then flew off.

Free as a bird, Jimmy thought, and he jerked at his trapped leg. Somehow, he had to get his foot free. But first he had better look at his arm. He rolled up the sleeve and carefully unwound the bandage. Fighting against the pain, he began to pick out a dozen tiny pieces of glass he had missed the night before. The wound began bleeding again, but it was a slow seepage rather than a flow, and Jimmy knew it would soon stop. Now that he could see what he was doing, he pressed the two sides of the cut together, then quickly wrapped the cut-off sleeve around the wound, tucking in the ends so his makeshift bandage would stay in place. Then he rolled his sleeve back down.

He looked out at the stream, some fifteen feet away, rushing through a bed of rounded boulders. The water bubbled and shot and leaped and burst into spray. The sight made him thirsty, but there was no way he could reach the stream. The water might as well be a mile away.

Minutes later he heard the sound of an approaching car and held his breath. Would the driver see those skid marks and stop to investigate? Then he remembered the horn, reached over, and pressed down on the silver ring. He heard a faint buzz but no other sound. The battery was dead, probably shorted out from a broken wire. The car passed the scene of the accident and moved away down the grade.

Jimmy looked at his watch — 6:35. That was the first car all morning. There wouldn't be much traffic. He had purposely taken a little-used gravel road because it was a shortcut of some twenty miles and also because the idea of driving along the dark tunnel of road through dense stands of ponderosa pine appealed to him. The scenery fitted his mood. The problem was that no one knew he had been on his way to visit his Uncle Carl. How would anyone know where to look for him?

When Jimmy had pulled into the parking lot at the Hourglass Lake picnic grounds for one of the graduation night parties, the first kid to spot him was Susan Hammer.

"Hey, Cracked, where's Charlene tonight?" she called out.

A dozen kids were sitting around a campfire. There was a chorus of greetings.

The kids called him "Cracked" because his name reminded them of the words of the old folk song, "Jimmy cracked corn and I don't care." For much the same reason his brother was called "Pop," and his sister, "Candy" Korne.

Jimmy had sat down beside Susan in the ring of kids. Someone was toasting marshmallows, and now he remembered he had brought a bag of marshmallows and some potatoes for the picnic. They should be in the back of the car.

"Charlene couldn't come?" Susan had asked.

"Aw, you know what juniors are like. They feel they're not wanted at graduation night parties."

"I bet she's resting up for Wayne," Susan said. "He's coming home on leave next week."

The news hit him like a blow in the pit of the stomach. For a moment he just sat there. Charlene had said nothing about Wayne coming home. Suddenly a whole lot of things fell into place. Wayne! So that was it.

Suddenly Jimmy stood up and began jogging back to the station wagon.

"Where are you going?" Susan yelled. "You just got here!"

He spun the wagon out of the parking lot and gunned the motor. Although he had two more graduation parties to go to, plus breakfast at the Milanos', he left the crowd at Hourglass Lake and sped back to town, desperate to get away from everyone for a while. At the public phone booth outside the V.F.W. hall, he called his uncle. Uncle Carl was a widower who sometimes went off to Seattle or Portland for a few days, but Jimmy got a busy signal and knew his uncle was at home. It was just after midnight. He had forty bucks and plenty of money for gas. He could make it in two hours.

Jimmy drove home and parked out on the street. Tiptoeing through the house, he grabbed his toilet kit, sleeping bag, and camera. For a moment he thought of leaving a note for his mother, but it didn't really matter. No one was expecting him until the next day, anyway. Carrying his gear, he left the house as silently as he had entered and didn't bother with the note.

He slid in behind the wheel. He'd reach his Uncle Carl's in a few hours. He would unroll the sleeping bag in the back of the wagon and sack out until Uncle Carl got up. Then he would call his mother and tell her where he was. Nobody would even need the car. His dad still had the pickup, and his mom had her Toyota. The 1968 Plymouth station wagon had been their family car years ago, but when Jimmy turned sixteen and got his license, he inherited it.

He thought of his family and imagined what they would say, if they knew where he was. His dad would probably drop some remark about the Great Klutz and then call his friends in the construction business, and they would cut him free of the car. And his brother Andy? If he knew "Pop," he would set up a little table on the side of the road and start selling tickets to visit his trapped brother down in the ravine. If there was a way to make a buck out of the situation, Andy would find it. The kid was amazing when it came to money. He already had over a thousand dollars socked away in the bank. Jimmy, on the other hand, never had more than a hundred dollars in his savings account. And Candy? What would she do? She'd probably bake him a batch of her chocolate chip cookies. And Charlene? He shook his head. He didn't even want to think of her now.

He heard the growling of gears as another vehicle came up the grade. By straining forward, Jimmy could just barely make out, through a gap in the trees, an empty logging truck.

"Stop," he muttered. "Please, stop."

But the vehicle rolled on and was eventually lost to sight. Despite his disappointment, he still felt sure that someone would soon notice those skid marks and stop to check them out. But he didn't realize that the car's roof blended in perfectly with the boulders and bushes on the streambed. Anyway, with all the trees that grew thickly on the banks of the ravine, very little of the roof was visible. And although Jimmy thought the skid marks from his car were highly visible, in fact there was only a scattered fan of gravel at the side of the road and a broken branch on a young pine nearby.

Jimmy turned now to his foot. If he could get

it loose, he could easily crawl out the window on the passenger's side or through the open windshield. Then he could cross the stream, drag himself up the slope, and stop a passing car. The crushed-in roof of the wagon did not give him enough room to sit up straight and reach his foot with either of his hands, but he was still able to see what was wrong. The front of the car had smashed into a tree stump or boulder with such force that the glove compartment had been crushed down around each side of his right ankle, pressing it to the floor, in effect locking his foot in a metal clamp. He did have some movement in the foot. He could turn it slightly to the left or right, but only a few inches. The metal arch fitted snugly around the ankle part of his hiking boot, as though it were a foot manacle. No bones seemed to be broken, and the only pain he felt was a scraping burn when he tried to turn his foot too far.

He felt like a coyote caught in a trap and fought against the panic that threatened to overwhelm him. It wasn't fair. He had been sure that with daylight he'd be able to figure out some way to get his foot free. But now, with a growing sense of despair, he began to realize that he might not be able to free that foot by himself. He jerked his leg savagely back and forth half a dozen times but only succeeded in hurting his ankle. He blinked back tears and fought to control himself. Panic wasn't going to help. There was no point in getting mad at the car or his foot. He had to face the fact that he was probably not going to get out of the vehicle on his own. He would just have to be patient and wait until someone found him.

Toward mid-morning he took the bandage off his arm to look at his wound again. The skin around the cut was now inflamed, and pus had started to form. He noticed several bits of glass he had missed, and despite the intense pain it caused, he managed to pick out the slivers with the tip of his knife. He was sweating when he finished. What made it worse was that he hated the sight of blood, especially his own.

He wondered what would happen if the arm got badly infected. If only he had some way to wash the wound. But the stream was too far away, and he had nothing to carry water in. He wondered where his toilet gear was. He had flung that and the camera on the front seat just after he left the house, but he couldn't find them now. They had probably fallen out of the shattered windshield when the car went bounding down the slope.

Jimmy refolded the makeshift bandage, then once again wrapped the arm and rolled down the sleeve to cover everything.

His folks might be out searching for him by now, if they'd spoken to any of his friends, but unfortunately, even if they did think of Uncle Carl, they wouldn't know he had taken the short-cut there. It was not the road he normally would have taken. Someone might eventually think of it, but he wouldn't bet on it. Even *he* had never taken that road before. And anyway, he had never actually gotten in touch with his uncle.

That afternoon another logging truck passed by, followed shortly by a car. Jimmy stuck his arm through the side window and beat his fist on the car, but no one heard him, and neither vehicle stopped. His thirst was now intense, and he decided he had to figure out some way of getting water from the stream. He couldn't think of anything, though. Maybe he would just have to tough it out until he was found. In the meantime, he decided to take a nap. He had hardly slept at all the night before.

Eyes closed, he began daydreaming about Charlene. He wondered if he were really in love with her. Sometimes he was sure he was; at other times, positive he wasn't. And how did she feel? She acted as though she really liked him, but lately she had been saying things like, "I'm not right for you, Jimmy" or "This is just a passing phase with us." It was as though she were trying to warn him not to take her seriously. Yet he knew he was the only one she went out with. Or at least he thought he was. She had been going steady with him ever since she broke up with Wayne over Christmas vacation. Wayne was already out of school, working at different jobs around town. Then early in January he had joined the Air Force and gone off for basic training in Texas somewhere. Charlene said she really didn't like Wayne, but she had gone out with him for over a year, and she still wore the silver-and-turquoise ring he had given her. The news that Wayne was coming home on leave had really jolted Jimmy. For one thing, it helped explain why Charlene had been acting so weird lately.

He dug around in the back pocket of his Levi's and pulled out his wallet to look at her picture. She was standing on the porch of her house, one arm up as though waving to someone. Her best feature, her eyes, were not really visible in the photo, as her face was shaded. Her high cheekbones, she said, came from a Cherokee great-grandmother, as did her long, straight black hair. Jimmy put the picture away and sighed.

He heard something pinging on the roof of the car. A scattered shower from the fringe of a nearby thunderstorm was passing through. The thunder sounded like a freight train rolling by in the distance.

Suddenly Jimmy sat up as much as the ceiling would allow. The thunderstorm had triggered off several violent pictures in his mind. What would happen if the creek flooded? And, a more horrifying possibility, suppose a forest fire were to start?

For the first time since the crash, the full helplessness of his situation swept over him, and he was seized with terror. He tugged desperately at his trapped foot.

"Help!" he screamed in panic. "Is anybody out there? Help! Please help me! I'm trapped!"

He kept yelling until his throat began to hurt and he was forced to stop. His heart pounded in his ears, and the harsh sound of his breathing blocked out all other noises.

"I don't want to die," he finally sobbed. "*I don't want to die!*"

Chapter Three

The night was endless. Every time Jimmy was about to fall asleep, he would hear a noise in the bushes that jerked him wide-awake. Was that a wild animal of some sort? Or just a stone rolling down the ravine? Then, too, his cramped position inside the car was awkward and uncomfortable. No matter what position he tried, something would eventually start hurting, and he would have to shift his body. The best he could do was doze off for five minutes at a time.

Once he heard a vehicle and saw a cone of light splay through the trees high above him. He shouted and banged the side of the car — to no avail. The night seemed to last a week. He kept hoping to see that light blue band in the eastern sky that meant dawn was approaching, and he checked his watch so often he began to wonder if something was wrong with it. Surely it had to be later than 2:00 in the morning. Finally, though, it was 5:30, and birds in the nearby trees began to announce the start of another day.

He looked around the inside of the wagon. He had wasted yesterday. Today he had to get organized. His first need was water. If he had water he could wash out that wound and take a drink. His mouth was dry and cottony, and he knew he wouldn't last more than a day or two without water, although he could do without food for a couple of weeks. . . . Food? Wait a minute, he *did* have food in the car! He had taken half a dozen baking potatoes and a bag of marshmallows to that picnic at Hourglass Lake. The food had been in a yellow plastic bucket somewhere in the back of the wagon. He hoped it hadn't fallen out like his toilet gear and camera had.

He craned his neck around and caught sight of the bucket jammed between the front and back seats on the passenger's side. By stretching his left arm, he was just able to grab the lip of the bucket and drag it toward him. Incredibly, the food was still in there, along with a roll of aluminum foil he had brought along to roast the potatoes. He opened the bag of marshmallows and ate half a dozen, then set aside the aluminum foil. Perhaps he could find some use for it later.

The marshmallows had only made his thirst worse. "Jimmy," he said aloud, "we have to get water somehow." "Yes, indeedy," he answered himself. "Just heave your old bucket into the stream and pull in a pail of that delicious water."

If only he could, Jimmy thought. He needed a rope to tie on the handle; then he would swing the bucket around his head a couple of times and let it fly. Sure, right out the window, right? Fat chance. He barely had room to scratch his ear, let along swing a bucket. What he needed was a long, flexible bamboo pole with a tin cup nailed to the end. Then he could scoop out a cup of water, and if he balanced the cup exactly right and was extremely careful drawing the pole back in through the window, he just might get a spoonful or two after the rest had sloshed out over the rim. It was hopeless. He would get water when someone found him and not before.

He spent the rest of the morning taking inventory of what was in the station wagon. He found a small collapsible fishing rod and a plastic tackle box. He could catch fish in the stream, if he could find some sort of bait. Boy, if his father could see him now, he would say his son didn't stand a snowball's chance in hell of getting out of the fix he was in. And he would be right, Jimmy thought mournfully. He just wasn't any good with his hands. Some guys had it, some guys didn't. He was one of the guys who didn't.

It was the same with girls. He just wasn't the kind of guy girls went for. Oh, sure, they liked him — he was good for a laugh — but they never really got passionate about him, not the way they did over guys like Wayne. Let's face it, why should they? He wasn't a jock. He wasn't terrific-looking. He wasn't exactly ugly, but as someone once said, he walked around as though he had an extra elbow or a third knee. And his nose was a disaster. The only thing he could say for himself was that he was good with animals.

Terrific, he loved animals. Who didn't? He wasn't a great student, either. At least, he never made the honor roll in school. He was a B-minus down the line, your average Joe. And a real disappointment to his dad. Jimmy didn't even like to hunt or fish. The collapsible rod was his dad's. He was more like Uncle Carl, who used to say of hunting and fishing, "Those poor critters never bothered me; why should I bother them?"

Jimmy strained to get another look at his foot. It was really locked in there. He would need a welding torch to cut his foot free, or one of those big jaws the cops use to straighten out bent metal.

He suddenly remembered that a whole bunch of other stuff was in the back somewhere. The old station wagon had a wheel-well on the side for the spare tire and another compartment under the floor. What was in that compartment? Jumper cables, he thought, and a box of tools and a lug wrench for removing the wheel to change a tire. If he could get that wrench out, maybe he could use it to pry the metal off his foot. But how was he going to get the compartment open? He couldn't even get his hand back that far, and if he could, the awkward angle of his body wouldn't give him enough leverage to lift the trapdoor. He shook his head, admitting defeat. Whatever was in the floor compartment was obviously going to stay there.

He turned his attention to the plastic tackle box, balancing it across his knees. Opening the lid, he looked at the contents: a packet of hooks, several small, brightly colored lures, a red plastic bobber, a dozen small lead weights, a tiny pair of pliers for straightening bent hooks, a piece of sandpaper. Not much he could use. He picked up one of the hooks. Could he attach it to the rod and sling it out the window and maybe snag some of those berries that were growing on a nearby bush? They didn't look ripe, though. In fact, they might not be edible; they could even be poisonous.

But despite his doubts, he decided to fish for berries. What else did he have to do? Working carefully, he attached a hook to the end of the nylon line on the fishing rod. He extended the rod to its full six feet, pushed it out the window, then flicked it so the lure sailed out into the bushes. He reeled it in. Nothing. But on his fifth or sixth cast he managed to snag a small bunch of berries and bring them inside the wagon. As he suspected, they were still hard and green. He threw them away. So much for that idea.

"Strike three!" he called out as the Great Klutz failed again.

He heard a car on the road above, and he waited for it to stop. There was no slackening in the sound of the engine, just a steady drone that finally died away. Again he wondered how he could signal to cars passing by on the road. He lifted the roll of aluminum foil. Could he unroll it out the window and hope the sun would shine off it? He didn't think that would work, somehow. Surely, though, he would be found by nightfall? It was just bad luck that he hadn't been found already. *Tonight, at the latest; by tomorrow noon at the very, very latest,* he assured himself.

He began to rummage through the contents of the demolished glove compartment, most of which had spilled out onto the floor. He noticed several road maps, plus a handful of clothespins. Could he use them in some way? In the back of the glove compartment he found a tire valve and a pencil. How about those? What he really needed was a flashlight. He lifted a pair of sunglasses from the floor. Could he somehow signal to cars with them? He didn't see how. Then he noticed the broken section of the folding rule again. Something about it disturbed him, though he couldn't say why. "Come on," he called out. "Can't you think of anything?"

He lay back and tried to relax. "I would like a quart of iced tea, followed by a quart of Pepsi, a quart of orange juice, and a quart of cold milk," he told an imaginary waitress.

Outside the window a small dark shape flashed through the underbrush, then showed up twenty yards away on top of a boulder, its tail flicking like the tip of a whip. It was a chipmunk.

"Here," Jimmy called. "Here, Chip, Chip, Chip." He began to daydream. He would entice the chipmunk inside the car and tame it with marshmallows. Then he would make a tiny barrel out of the tire valve and tie it around the chipmunk's neck. Chip would then race to the stream, fill the barrel, and bring it back to him. Much later, after he was rescued, he and Chip would appear on *That's Incredible*, giving a demonstration of their lifesaving methods.

Another flash, and the chipmunk disappeared. But the sight of that flicking tail had stirred an image in Jimmy's mind. He had a fishing rod, right? If he could tie a rag to the line, then toss it into the stream, the rag would soak up water, and he could draw it back to the station wagon and maybe wring out enough for a drink.

But first he needed to rest.

CHAPTER FOUR

Jimmy surprised himself by sleeping for over an hour early that afternoon. He awoke when he heard a car approaching. "Come on," he murmured. "Come on, slow down, huh? Please, slow down and see the skid marks. Okay, now you're slowing . . ." But the car wasn't slowing.

"Help!" Jimmy screamed as loudly as he could, banging the outside of the door.

Finally he gave up and turned back to the problem of getting water. He was unbearably thirsty — his tongue seemed to be clogging his throat, and the roof of his mouth felt like sandpaper. He needed a rag to tie on the lure. *Think!* If he cut off his other shirt-sleeve he would have nothing to roll down over the arm to keep dirt away from the wound. *Come on, think!* A rag, a cloth of some kind.

He poked at the sleeping bag. What would happen if he cut some of the liner out? He stuck the blade of his knife in and made a small cut. Another piece of cloth was underneath, holding the fiberfill insulation in place. He widened the slit and soon had cut a piece the size of a hand towel from the sleeping-bag liner.

Working carefully, he fastened the rag to the hook. Then he eased the rod through the window. He gave his wrist as strong an upward flick as he could and watched the rag and line sail out some ten feet, but it wasn't close enough. He reeled in, being careful not to catch the lure on any undergrowth. After several casts, he was able to drop the rag into a small pool on the near side of the creek.

He let it sit there awhile, soaking up water, then began to reel it in. He swore when it got caught between two small rocks, but he worked it out of the rocky cleft and dragged it carefully toward him over the ground. Despite his caution, the rag slid through a patch of sand and gravel, but he couldn't worry about that. Pulling the rod backward, he got it inside, then lifted the soaking rag to his mouth. Gratefully he sucked the water, trying to avoid the bits of sand. He spat out several grains, then once more baited the hook and poked the rod out the window to repeat the whole process. It took him a good ten minutes for each cast and retrieve, and an hour must have passed before he had drunk enough water to satisfy his thirst. He then made a cast with a fresh piece of rag and used it to wash out his cut. The wound seemed no worse, though he had to spend several minutes teasing a few more bits of glass out of the raw flesh with the blade of his knife. However, it hurt so much he was soon forced to stop. He still hadn't gotten them all out, he knew. He washed the cut as best he could, gasping when he touched a sensitive spot, then bandaged the wound again.

Over the course of the next several hours, five vehicles passed by on the road. Each time, Jimmy shouted and banged away, but each time the car drove on without even slowing down. Obviously no one could hear him. He had to find some better way to signal passing cars. But how?

"Come on, think of something," he urged himself.

But it was no good; he was fresh out of ideas. And now, for the first time, he seriously considered the possibility that he would never get out of the wrecked car, that no one would find him. Years from now someone would stumble across his skeleton. Boy, wouldn't Charlene be sorry then? He gave a shudder and began yanking on his trapped leg. "*I don't want to die,*" he repeated desperately to himself. And then, "*Somebody help me! Please!*"

His panic finally passed, and he began to calm down. It wasn't over yet, he reminded himself. After all, he had discovered a way to get water. And he had food. He reached down and dragged out the potatoes and marshmallows. He had six potatoes. Okay, so they were raw and he had no way of cooking them. But weren't they just as good raw, as far as food value went? Maybe even better; the skins were supposed to contain certain minerals and vitamins. The marshmallows weren't too useful, though, just sugar really, but every little bit helped. He took them all out of the bag and counted them—seventy-four. Then he looked at his watch. It was 2:30. He hadn't eaten anything for breakfast. Now he decided to eat part of a potato. With his knife, he sliced an oblong one in half and put the other half back in the bag. He began to eat, cutting tiny slices off as though it were an apple. He realized it was the first time he had ever eaten a raw potato.

Jimmy finished the potato half and ate five marshmallows. Who would ever have thought a raw potato could taste so delicious? What was it his Uncle Carl used to say? "Hunger makes the best sauce!" He smiled as he thought of his uncle and all his funny sayings. "Never do today what you can put off until tomorrow" and "The early bird catches pneumonia."

After his lunch, he decided to start a diary. He thought he should record what he was going through. But what could he use for paper? Scrounging around among the road maps, he came upon a small pad of printed receipt slips that his dad used. He could write on the backs of them. He pulled one off. There was even a line for the date, but what date was it? Let's see, he crashed on Sunday, Graduation Day, the

29th of June. Boy, he wouldn't forget that date in a hurry. Monday, then, was the 30th and today had to be the first of July.

"Oh, Great Klutz," he said. "Today is the first of July. Only twelve more days to your birthday."

He filled in the date and turned the slip over, then took a minute to sharpen the pencil with his knife. What should he put down? "Have food and water but can't get out of here," he wrote. "Foot caught and right arm cut. Sunny, warm, but no cars stopping. Miss everybody, especially you, Charlene."

Folding the slip of paper carefully, he slid it into his wallet. Now what? Perhaps he should continue trying to figure out a way to signal passing cars.

But he lapsed into daydreams instead and found himself thinking about an incident with Charlene. He had been having a slice of pizza with her at the Pizza House when suddenly she asked, out of the clear blue, if soldiers could get married.

Jimmy had never thought about it and had no idea. "I guess so," he finally said. "Why?"

"It was something I saw on television," Charlene replied. "There was this soldier who said he was going to get married as soon as he went on leave. I thought soldiers couldn't get married. I mean, they can get killed in a war, right?"

"Maybe they have to be a certain age, like twenty-five, or something."

"Oh, you think so?" She looked alarmed for a

moment, then seemed to forget about it, saying, "Connie is going to buy a car, a real neat Volkswagen."

Why had she seemed upset? Jimmy wondered. That was the big problem with him — he just didn't understand girls. Maybe that's why he was so good with animals. That same day he had fixed a starling's wing. Boy, that was something! He had never known such a good feeling in his life. It was about the only time his dad had ever been impressed with him.

Jimmy had found the bird hopping around awkwardly in the backyard, unable to fly, one wing stuck out at an odd angle. Placing a bath towel over it, he managed to capture it and bring it inside the house. Then he put the starling in a large cardboard box, along with a saucer of water, and covered the box with chicken wire. That afternoon when his dad came home from work, he had shown him the starling.

"Better kill it, son," his father had said. "With a wing like that, it just can't survive. Some cat will only mangle it to death."

"Maybe I can fix the wing," Jimmy suggested.

His father laughed gently. "Oh, sure. My son, the surgeon."

"Maybe I *can* fix it," Jimmy repeated stubbornly. "Then teach it to talk. Starlings can be trained to talk. Did you know that, Dad?"

"Just teach it to fly again," his father had said. "That'll be plenty."

Later, when his father was watching the news

on television, Jimmy took the bird outside and examined it. Carefully he felt the first joint of the wing. It seemed to be loose or something. As gently as he could, he folded the broken wing into the same position as the other wing. The bird began to struggle, and soon the wing was jutting out again at that awkward angle. Once more Jimmy eased the wing back into place and then brought the starling and box down to the basement. Cutting strips off an old T-shirt and using the broken-off wings of a plastic model airplane, he made a crude brace for the bird's wing and wrapped the whole thing with cloth and tape. Then he left the bird down in the basement.

Several days later, he removed the bandage, lifted the bird out of the box, and set it on the table. The starling took a few hesitant steps. It didn't seem to know it was free. Jimmy reached for it, and the bird lunged off the table and dropped to the lawn, where it hopped around in a circle. Jimmy felt a quick stab of pity. He hadn't been able to help the bird after all. He bent down, intending to put it back in the box, and suddenly it ran forward a few steps and lifted into the air. It flapped a few times and landed in an oak tree.

"It can fly!" Jimmy screamed. He kept yelling, and his mother ran outside to see what was wrong.

"Mom, I healed the bird. It just flew off!"

He pointed to where the starling was sitting on

a branch, grooming its wings. As they watched, it took off and swooped low across the yard to land in another tree.

"He's all right!" Jimmy shouted. He felt wonderful! He had set a bird's wing and made it whole again.

Later Jimmy realized that the wing was probably only sprained or out of joint and that the bird would have recovered on its own. But he had still saved its life. The starling might not have recovered before a dog or cat got to it.

When his father came home from work that evening, he was impressed when Jimmy told him about the starling. "Well, I know where to go if I ever break a wing," he joked. "Good work. I would have said that bird was a dead duck."

"You *did* say it," Jimmy pointed out.

He heard a pinging noise on the roof, and it jerked him back to reality.

He had to concentrate, had to find a way of attracting the attention of drivers going by on the road. Already three vehicles had passed today. But what could he do? Make a fire? Or wave a sheet of aluminum foil? How about sig-signaling with the rearview mirror on the passenger's side?

He sat forward and stretched an arm out the front window. Thank God the mirror hadn't broken off. It was bent, but still intact, the glass hardly even cracked. He could just barely touch the bracket. If he could grab the whole bracket, he could probably rock it back and forth until it broke free, but he couldn't reach far enough. It was hopeless.

He slumped back. The Great Klutz had failed again.

CHAPTER FIVE

Jimmy spent the rest of the afternoon trying to figure out a way to make a signal. For supper he ate five marshmallows and half a potato. Waiting through the night was the worst part. With nothing to see or do, his thoughts naturally turned to home. He kept trying to picture what everyone was doing. Of course, now that he was missing, they'd probably all be out looking for him, even Grungy, his dog.

An unbearable loneliness swept over him, and he wanted to cry. "Oh, Mom! Oh, Dad!" he called softly into the dark. They were always there when he needed them. It was terrifying to know that they couldn't come to him now, that maybe he would die there in the car without ever seeing them again. Surely that couldn't happen . . . could it?

He buried his head in the sleeping bag, and mercifully, he dozed off. Several times he heard cars or trucks passing and could even see their headlights, but he didn't expect them to stop at night, and they drove on, their lights finally disappearing. If there were only some way he could signal with a light. Then he thought of something. If he could see their lights, maybe they could see a light down in the ravine. He could flash signals, like the SOS in Morse code: three longs, three shorts, three longs. He had to get into the storage compartment in the back, figure out a way to lift that lid. Maybe the flashlight was in there.

At first light in the morning he decided to work the plastic bucket over to the stream and capture water in the pail rather than by casting the rag. If he could pull in a quarter of a bucket of water, he would save a lot of time and effort.

He hooked the handle of the bucket on two hooks on the fishing line, then half-bounced, half-cast the bucket toward the stream. Finally he managed to tumble the yellow pail into the nearest pool and partially fill it with water. But when he tried to pull it back, the bucket weighed so much he was sure the fishing line would break under the strain. He reeled in as much as he dared, then pulled on the rod itself. The line arched and the bucket half-lifted, but the strain on the line was too much. He pulled again, and suddenly the rod flew back to him. Great. Something had broken. The wire handle of the pail had popped free of its brackets. He pulled the rod and handle in. He had lost his bucket, he thought, but at least he had saved the handle. He might even find a use for it — maybe he could bend it into a big hook of some kind and snag grass or berries with it. He set the handle aside and looked out at the bucket. It had fallen back into the pool and was now already half full of water. He wasn't going to get it back, that was for sure.

For a while he was angry with himself. He had acted foolishly and had lost his only bucket. Casting with the rod had worked well enough, so why did he want to improve it? He couldn't afford to lose anything or do anything stupid. His margin of survival was too thin. What did Uncle Carl say about that old army rule? "If something works, don't fix it."

He went back to the problem of signaling cars on the road. Maybe he could wad up bits of aluminum foil and throw them out the window. The sun, reflecting off the shiny surface, might make someone stop and then notice the car down in the ravine. But wait a minute, wasn't he going off half-cocked again? The balls of foil would only be blown away by the wind, and besides, they'd be so small.

How about the outside mirror? To get it off, he would need tools. The tools and maybe the flashlight were in the floor compartment, but he couldn't lift the trapdoor. Somehow he had to find a way to get it open.

He turned on his side and maneuvered the hook on the end of the rod into the shallow ring at the back of the trapdoor, trying to catch the hook, so he could pull the door up. It took almost an hour to work the hook into the ring, but at last he did it. He reeled in until the line went taut.

"Okay, Great Klutz, here we go!" he said.

He began turning the reel. The door lifted almost an inch. With the rod jammed under his body, he continued to reel in, and the door kept rising, though he expected the line to snap at any moment. Finally the door was open several inches. Now he had to keep it that way. He couldn't reach the metal rod that was normally used for propping the door open, but he thought of something else. He dropped the plumber's helper down into the well. Holding his breath, he cautiously let the weight of the door ease down onto the end of the wooden handle.

He let out a shout. He had done it! The trapdoor was now propped open, and he could get at the toolbox.

"Oh, Great Klutz, you were magnificent!" he said.

He snagged the toolbox and pulled it into his lap. When he opened the lid, he found an assortment of small wrenches, three or four screwdrivers, including a stubby and a Phillips, two pairs of pliers, three spark plugs, a pack of ignition wrenches, and a handful of bolts, nuts, washers, and split pins. There wasn't a whole lot he could use, though maybe the screwdrivers would come in handy. He had been hoping to find something like a hammer or a pry bar that would help him remove that outside mirror. And he had especially been hoping to find a flashlight.

However, he turned his attention to the mirror and got to work with the Phillips screwdriver. Because of the cut on his arm, he found it difficult to exert much pressure on the screw. No matter how he tried, he couldn't budge it. After half an hour of exhausting attempts, he gave up and lay back on the sleeping bag.

He rested briefly, then decided to try to get the lug wrench out of the floor compartment. He half-turned, twisted his head, and fished in the well with the bucket handle. Little by little he raked the wrench toward him until he was able to pull it in and examine it. He hefted it in his hand. It was solid and would make a good, rackety noise. Pushing his arm through the window, he banged half a dozen times on the car door. The air in the ravine rang with the sound of the blows. If a car stopped above, the driver would surely hear the sound. But first he had to find a way to make someone stop and get out of the car.

He set the lug wrench down. All that work had made him hungry. He pulled out the bag of potatoes and ate one, cutting tiny slices off one end and chewing them thoroughly. He finished the meal with three marshmallows. Then he felt around on the floor for his pencil and found instead the section of the carpenter's folding rule. He ran his finger over the numbers and the brass tip at one end of the hinge. The section had broken at the hinge, and he could just picture his dad swearing when the rule broke. Jimmy closed his eyes and suddenly had a horrible vision of a red face looming over him, its mouth raw and roaring. His eyes flew open, and he shook his head. That was all he needed, to start having nightmares in the middle of the day!

He put the broken rule in the toolbox and continued searching for the pencil. When he found it, he tore a slip of paper off the receipt pad and wrote, "Wednesday, July 2." On the back of the slip he made his diary entry: "Several cars passed. Got toolbox and lug wrench out of well. Itchy all over, and arms still hurt, but otherwise okay. Can't give up."

After he put the folded slip away in his wallet, he lay back to take a nap. He woke sometime later to the sound of a car.

"This one's it!" he shouted. He snatched up the lug wrench, stuck his arm out the window, and banged furiously on the side of the car. "Please notice me," he said. And then, "Please, God, make him stop," he prayed over and over as he banged away with the wrench and the sound of the car died in the distance. That must have been the twentieth car that had passed since the crash, and not one of the drivers had noticed anything wrong. He felt a quick flash of anger at them for being so blind. What did they need before they would stop — a huge sign in the middle of the road, "MAN TRAPPED IN CANYON BELOW"?

He wondered about his family. They must be going nuts at home, especially his mother. They'd all be out looking for him, but they wouldn't know where to search. His dad might even think he had run away from home. Less than a week ago he had kidded around about heading for Alaska to live in the wilderness. Maybe they would think he had run off without telling anyone. The whole thing had come just after an argument with his father, who wanted him to go into the family business after graduation. His dad was really something. First he'd claim his oldest son wasn't able to do anything with his hands. Then he'd say he wanted Jimmy to go into the contracting business. "I can use you painting," his dad said. "You can make good money with me."

But that wasn't what Jimmy wanted to do with his life. He wanted to work with animals, maybe get a job in a stable or an animal hospital. What he wanted to do was become a veterinarian, but his grades weren't good enough. Anyway, he'd still like to try working with animals for a year or so, just to see how he liked it.

The big problem with his dad was that Jimmy couldn't work with him. His father was too impatient, and everything had to be done just right, *his* way. He was a perfectionist. And no matter what Jimmy did, his dad did it over.

Practically nothing he had ever done had pleased his father. He remembered once, back in the seventh grade, bringing home a small walnut box from school. Okay, so he had had some help with it from the shop teacher, but he was still proud of it. What did the perfectionist say? "It's a good job, but that dovetail joint could be tighter. And you didn't countersink the screws enough."

He had practically burst into tears. It was the best thing he had ever made, and he had looked forward to showing it off, but his dad found fault with everything he did. The odd thing was, the guys who worked for him in the business didn't get that treatment. And Andy — who wasn't any genius with his hands, either — never got picked on. Maybe that was because Andy was clever, always figuring out a way to make an extra buck, and his dad admired that. It didn't make any difference that Andy wasn't that good at building things. As his dad once said, "When you got the smarts, you don't need brawn. But when you don't got either, you got trouble." Jimmy was sure he had been a big disappointment to his father.

A rustle in the undergrowth drew his attention. A chipmunk was standing on its hind legs, its little tail sticking straight up.

"Here, Chip, Chip, Chip," Jimmy called.

Suddenly, out of nowhere, a second chipmunk appeared, chattering away at him.

"Yeah, I know, you guys are wondering what I'm doing in here," he said. "Come on, I'll feed you a bit of marshmallow."

He held a piece of marshmallow out the window, but the pair wouldn't come any closer. He made kissing sounds with his lips, and one of them advanced a few quick, skittery steps, then raced back.

Maybe he could tame them, if he had enough time. He could always get chickadees to come down and feed from his hand. He bet he could do the same with the chipmunks. He threw a piece of marshmallow out the window. To his surprise, one of the chipmunks grabbed it and began to nibble on it.

For quite a while he played with the chipmunks, trying to entice them closer. He kept throwing out tiny bits of marshmallow, dropping each one closer to the car until the two animals were within arm's reach. He wasted three whole marshmallows, but he didn't mind. The company was well worth it, and it gave him a way to pass the time.

Finally the chipmunks disappeared. Then the light slowly faded in the western sky, and he was faced with another long, bleak night to get through — somehow.

Chapter Six

Jimmy's night was shot through with disturbing dreams. In one, he argued violently with a truck driver who had appeared in his family's driveway pulling a flatbed trailer piled high with wooden beams he wanted to unload. Jimmy knew his dad hadn't ordered the lumber and tried to convince the driver to take his wood somewhere else, but the driver pulled some sort of a lever on his truck and the beams started to slide off. "It's too late," the driver said. "The load is spilled. You'll *have* to buy it now."

In another dream an awesome atomic fireball rose above his town. Then it turned out to be some sort of volcanic eruption that was going to engulf everyone.

Never was the dawn more welcome. When it finally came, Jimmy groaned as he moved his body around. He was stiff all over, not only from his awkward sleeping position, but also from the dozen aches and pains he had suffered in the crash.

He rolled up his right sleeve, took the bandage

off, and looked at the cut. Although it seemed to be healing all right, he decided to wash it again. Casting with the fishing rod, he soaked a piece of liner in the stream and then bathed his wound with the wet cloth. He found another tiny sliver of glass and, gritting his teeth against the pain, teased it out with his knife. As the cut healed it seemed to be forcing bits of glass to the surface. Pressing both sides of the cut together as closely as he could, Jimmy wound the bandage tightly around his arm and then rolled down the sleeve of his shirt.

What was funny was that he couldn't remember actually cutting his arm. He had felt the blows all right, but not any pain until five minutes after the car had come to rest. He had probably been in shock.

He dug around for the receipt pad and made another entry in his diary: "July 3. Tomorrow big holiday. Still no sign of rescue. Three or four cars passed. Made friends with two chipmunks."

While he had the wallet out, he withdrew the picture of Charlene. "Well, Charl, what are you thinking about right now?" he asked. "I bet it's not me, is it? I bet you're planning how to spend those two or three weeks with Wayne."

He ate another potato half and two marshmallows, then cast for his usual morning drink. After that he dug out the lug wrench and wondered if he could use it to pry the metal off his foot. Leaning forward, he was able to jam the screwdriver end of the wrench between the piece of metal and the floor. He tried levering upward, but the position of his body gave him no power in his arms or shoulders. Also, he was trying to force the metal up and into the framework of the dashboard, which meant he was trying to lift the whole car. He would be better off trying to force the metal sideways, to spread the wings of the collar, but that seemed impossible, too. He had nothing to brace the handle against. About the only thing that would work would be a backsaw blade or an acetylene torch.

By noon, after several vehicles had passed by, Jimmy made an important decision. It was now his fourth day trapped in the car and no one on the road had noticed anything wrong. He would either have to find a better way to draw attention to his plight, or he would have to free himself from the car. Time was running out.

He turned once again to the outside mirror. Digging the end of the lug wrench between the mirror arm and the car door, he pried outward and upward. The mirror moved an inch or so. He pried some more until he had straightened the mirror out to its original position, but it wouldn't move any farther. He couldn't work it back, either, without hitting it with something, which might break the glass. He looked through the toolbox for the Phillips screwdriver. Setting the end of the screwdriver in the crossnotch of the screw head, he tapped the handle with the wrench. The screw turned a fraction. Half a dozen taps with the wrench and the screw was turning easily. In a few minutes he was holding the mirror in his hand. Now he had something to signal with! The only problem was that the sun was hidden behind clouds. But once he had sun, he was convinced the mirror would bring him help. Bouncing the reflection off someone's eyes would surely make him or her stop to see what was causing it.

Sometime around noon the two chipmunks showed up, and he threw them some more marshmallow. This time he was able to entice them closer and closer to the car window, until one of them actually came within a couple of inches of his outstretched fingers. Then, as though amazed at its bravery, the chipmunk scampered back and rejoined its mate. Jimmy decided to name them. The larger and more venturesome one he called "Flash" after a German shepherd his family had once owned. The other he named "Trigger" after a terrier that belonged to a neighbor.

Thinking of Flash and Trigger reminded him of Grungy, the dog his family owned now. Jimmy had found her starving and abandoned in the woods, and he had coaxed her into friendship with food. Someone must have beaten her at one time, because she was afraid of everyone. It took weeks of tender care before she didn't cringe whenever someone went near her.

Jimmy was the only one she really trusted. At first his dad didn't want him to keep her. He was afraid she might be carrying some disease, and he was the one who had named her Grungy, because of her dirty, unkempt appearance. But

Jimmy loved her. He could tell she really needed someone to be good to her. Okay, she wasn't the sort of dog who would rush into a burning building and save your life, but so what? All dogs didn't have to be Lassie. Anyway, the vet had okayed her, and in time his dad came around and now loved Grungy as much as everyone else in the family did.

Jimmy's thoughts drifted to Charlene. Funny how he had started going out with her, he thought. It all had begun several weeks before Wayne joined the Air Force. Charlene had called Jimmy one evening and asked if he was taking his car on the field trip to Quincey Meadows. It was a combined trip for two classes, and the kids could ride in the school bus if they wanted to, but they could also go in their own cars. He hadn't thought about taking his car, but when Charlene asked if she could ride with him, he jumped at the chance.

All that day at the Meadows she had stuck to him, teasing him, fooling around, so it was only natural for him to ask her to have a Coke and hamburger when they were on their way home. What he hadn't expected, though, was to run into Wayne at the diner. As soon as she spotted Wayne, Charlene had gotten even more friendly with Jimmy, linking arms with him and dropping her head to his shoulder now and again. He had been embarrassed for Wayne. Obviously it was all over between him and Charlene, and several weeks later he heard that Wayne had gone off and joined the Air Force. He didn't mind getting her on the rebound. In fact, he had fallen in love with her before their next date was over. Of course he was cool about it, but she had to have some idea of how he felt. It was certainly obvious to others. Susan had said to him once, "Boy, you're really off the wall over that one."

Lying back on the broken seat, he looked through the window and up at the road. If the sun would only come out, he could use the mirror. *How about noise?* he wondered. What sort of loud noise could he make? The horn didn't work anymore. It was a pity the radio didn't play. It had broken years ago, and no one had ever bothered to fix it. It would have been nice to listen to some music, or even the news. There might even be bulletins out about him! He could imagine the announcements: "Mysterious disappearance of youth on graduation night. Frantic family appeals for help. Thousands join search."

He turned on one hip, putting a strain on his trapped leg. He worried about cutting off the circulation in his foot, but so far it felt fine. He wagged it from side to side every now and again. Obviously the flow of blood wasn't affected.

Tomorrow, he thought, *the sun will come out and I'll be rescued.* Tomorrow was Independence Day. With a big Fourth of July weekend coming up, there should be a lot more tourists on the road, a lot more traffic passing through.

He would be able to stop one of the cars with his mirror. Or maybe a car would overheat, and the driver would have to hike down to the creek for water. Maybe some family would stop and decide to picnic down by the stream. Maybe his Uncle Carl would come along in a helicopter, drop a long steel cable, and lift the car up to the road. Maybe the accident would reverse itself, his arm magically heal, the car straighten out all its dents, the windows become whole again as the wagon floated up and out of the canyon and landed on the road and that deer jumped backward over the hood, like a scene reversing itself in the movies.

Full of maybes, he drifted in and out of sleep as darkness fell and the night closed in around him.

Chapter Seven

Early the next morning Jimmy awoke to find Flash and Trigger scampering around in the front seat of the car. He fed them half a marsh-mallow, and they ventured quite close to his out-stretched fingers, but then he decided he couldn't afford to waste any more marshmallows that day.

One good thing, Jimmy thought, was that the weather had cleared somewhat. It was a partially sunny day, with only scattered clouds. He stretched the mirror out the window and experi-mentally flashed it toward the road. If he had a long stick of some kind, he could tie the mirror to the end of it and reach that much farther out the window. But what could he use?

He spent the next half hour tying the mirror across the rubber cup of the plumber's helper with a few yards of nylon line that he stripped off the fishing reel. It was shaky, but it might do. Cautiously he eased the handle out the window and found it easy to tilt the mirror. Then he withdrew the mirror and put the contraption on the front seat behind the steering wheel. He would use it later.

Now what? He checked his watch. It was almost 10:30, on the morning of the Fourth of July. The usual July Fourth parade would be going on at home, he thought, with the high school band and the Boy Scouts and the Girl Scouts and the American Legion and everything. They would be all jumbled around the cemetery at one end of town, where the parade always started. Old "Marker" Quinn would be carrying the flag. Marker was a World War II veteran who got his nickname from carrying the yard markers at all the high school football games. Suddenly Jimmy felt an aching loneliness for everyone at home.

After ten minutes of missing everyone and feeling sorry for himself, Jimmy pushed the fishing rod out the window and lofted the rag lure toward the stream. Several casts and he had his morning drink. The yellow bucket was still out there, wedged between two rounded boulders. He ought to try to get it back, even though he didn't have any particular use for it at the moment. He cast several times with the artificial lure, hoping to snag the lip of the bucket, but without any luck. Finally he cast his cleaning rag and brought it back to wash out his wound. This time he found no glass. Perhaps he had finally gotten it all out. It seemed to be healing nicely, though it was hard to tell. The important thing was to keep the bandage tight and the wound free of dirt. So far he'd been able to do that. It was still painful to touch, though, especially when he was washing it.

By 11:30, the sunshine was strong, and Jimmy pushed the plumber's helper out the window. The light bounced off the glass, and he began manipulating the handle to cast the beam up toward the road. Now all he needed was a car. At 11:50, one came down the grade, and he directed the flash up through the trees to the road. The pale, circular patch of light glanced off tree trunks, flashed briefly off a chrone bumper, then went sliding along the hood to bounce off the windshield in an explosion of light.

Jimmy could hardly contain himself and let out a whhop of joy. "All right!"

He had done it. See? The car was slowing down. He was finally going to be rescued. No way could the driver ignore that intense beam of light. It must have practically blinded him. He waited confidently for the driver to pull up, but the car continued on down the grade, and finally, unbelievingly, Jimmy could hear it no more. For five minutes he kidded himself that the car had stopped and the driver was out searching the road for whatever had almost caused him to crash. But finally he gave up hope.

Why hadn't the mirror worked? He was positive he had flashed the light straight into the driver's eyes. Perhaps the car had some sort of tinted windshield that blocked the light. Or maybe the driver thought the flash came from a puddle or stream. Or maybe he had just ignored it.

Though bitterly disappointed, Jimmy refused to give up hope. The mirror worked, there was no question of that. The next passing vehicle would stop and help him. The first car had been only a practice run. *Coming up, the real thing!* he thought to himself. His hand out the window, he waited. Every few minutes he held his breath to listen intently, desperately trying to pick up the sound of an approaching car. At 1:30 he heard a faint, irregular murmur in the distance, a sound that grew into the whine of a truck in low gear, its tires crunching a coarse static from the rough gravel.

A large pickup with a camper cab nosed into view around a curve. Jimmy saw it while it was still some distance away, and he was able to direct the flash of sunlight directly in the path of the truck. Holding his breath and listening hard, Jimmy waited for the vehicle to slow down and stop, perhaps even go into reverse.

Again the sound continued on down the road and died away into silence. And again Jimmy tried to kid himself that the driver had stopped and was backtracking on foot, trying to find the source of that flashing beam of light. But after ten minutes he knew that the driver had simply paid no attention.

He gave up for a while and eased the mirror back in through the window. Then he lay in his resting position, his head pillowed on the sleeping bag. What did he have to do to attract attention, he wondered angrily — set off a bomb?

Face it, he told himself. It looked as though he

would never be rescued. And he couldn't get out by himself. He would probably die right there, and Charlene would probably not care one bit. It was pretty obvious she had only been using him. What must have happened was that she and Wayne had had a big fight over something, and Wayne went off and enlisted just to show her he didn't care.

So Charlene decided to give Wayne something to think about by going out with Jimmy. Come to think of it, several of Jimmy's dates with Charlene had been at the Playmore Bowling Alley, where Wayne's sister worked as a waitress. Why hadn't he thought of it before? Charlene had suggested going there. She must have been hoping Gail would pass the word on to her brother. *So there, Wayne, eat your heart out, old Charlene is having a good time, don't you worry..*

He groaned. Now, on top of everything else, he had a raging headache. It probably came from all that rich food he wasn't eating. Oh, for a Big Mac with a sesame seed bun, a chocolate milk shake, a double order of French fries, and then on to Dairy Queen for a Banana Blizzard! Two long banana halves buried under four scoops of ice cream, two chocolate and two vanilla, drowned in chocolate sauce, smothered in whipped cream, sprinkled with nuts and dusted with sprinkles and topped off with a cherry — it hurt just to think of it.

He reached under the seat, took out a new potato, cut off a thin slice, and began to chew.

Some Big Mac, some Banana Blizzard, some Fourth of July.

"Oh, Great Klutz, it's Friday the Fourth. Let's celebrate!" he wailed aloud. The Great Klutz said nothing. This was his fifth day of being trapped, and he was no closer to getting out than he had been on the first. He should have realized that the flashing mirror wasn't such a great idea. It was a thousand-to-one shot he would be rescued because someone noticed a bright flash. That sort of thing happened in the movies, but in real life people couldn't be bothered about a temporary flicker of light in their eyes.

Trying to free his foot hadn't worked, either. Nothing had worked, except getting water from the stream. Andy would have been out of there inside of twenty-four hours and then would have sold his story to the newspapers and TV for several thousand dollars. Still, he didn't really want to be like Andy. Maybe he should be more like his sister. She was a lot better balanced.

Jimmy dug around in his back pocket and pulled out his wallet. Then, taking one of the receipts, he filled in the date, turned to the blank side, and wrote: "Mirror no good. Now 5 days here. July 4. Independence, where are you?" He folded the slip, put it away in his wallet, and lay back down again.

For the next hour, while listening for cars, he reached his arm as far out the window as he could and plucked long stalks of wild grass. It tasted faintly of gasoline, but he ate it anyway, chewing until only a few stringy fibers were left, and he spat them out.

He had been trying to eat something green every day if he could, to supply his body with vitamin C and other nutrients. Of course, it wasn't really enough, though, and after a while there would be nothing left to pick out there — unless he was somehow able to extend his reach.

After his "salad" he went back to experimenting with the lug wrench. Although he couldn't shift the metal collar away from his foot, it might be possible to cut through it with a chisel. But he didn't have a chisel. For that matter, he didn't have a hammer to hit a chisel with, so that idea was hopeless, too. He poked one end of the lug wrench into the fold of metal just above his ankle and tried to widen the area by prying outward. As before, he had no effect on the metal. He needed something to act as a fulcrum or wedge, something for the wrench to work off.

Tomorrow was Saturday. Surely plenty of traffic would be going by on the road above? On the other hand, he would lose most of the commercial traffic on Saturday; there wouldn't be any logging trucks or highway department vehicles or forest service pickups on the road.

The image of a flag floating up above the roof of his wagon suddenly popped into his mind. Independence Day and all that. Could someone see a flag from the road? Could a flag be a signal? What could he use? His denim jacket? It wasn't noticeable enough. How about that roll of aluminum foil? If he could make some sort of stiff flag, backed with aluminum foil, he could somehow stick it up on the roof of the wagon. It was worth a try. But what could he use for backing? He looked around. Why not the ceiling liner? Some of it had already sprung loose, and he could easily rip a section out.

Faced with a new problem to solve, he began to feel better. He'd figure out some way of using the ceiling liner to make a flag. Maybe this time he had the answer!

CHAPTER EIGHT

On Saturday morning the sky was overcast, which meant Jimmy couldn't use the mirror. He killed an hour getting his usual morning drink, cleaning and inspecting his wound, and eating a breakfast of half a potato and two marshmallows. He was especially careful now about cleanliness, washing his face and hands, his ears and neck, and whatever parts of his body he could reach with a piece of wet sleeping-bag liner. His body wastes were another problem. There was nothing he could do about the urine, except make sure he didn't get any on his clothes or sleeping bag. Twice he had to wrap his excreta in aluminum foil and heave it out the window. Despite his care, the place was beginning to smell. There was nothing he could do about it, though.

He also ran through a short series of physical exercises every now and then: reaching forward as far as he could, then leaning back; twisting his torso from side to side; doubling and extending his free leg a dozen times; flexing the biceps in both arms. He even tried to exercise his trapped foot, contracting and extending the toes in addition to rotating the ankle as much as the metal collar would allow.

Then, for the next several hours that morning, he worked on cutting a rough square out of a piece of ceiling liner that he had pulled down the evening before. The material was plastic and took a long time to cut with the big blade of his knife, but finally he had made a rectangular piece, roughly sixteen by twelve inches. He now set about attaching the foil to one side of his makeshift flag. He had no glue, but he did have six clothespins. He dug out the roll of aluminum foil and cut a piece large enough to cover one side of his piece of liner. Then he attached the foil with the clothespins. It seemed to hold.

Handling his flag as carefully as he could, Jimmy eased it out the window and let it slide down until it was propped against the outside of the car. Perhaps the sun, when it came out, would strike off the shiny surface and cause someone to investigate the strange flash. Surely that much silver surface would be partially visible from the road? His original plan had been to fly the flag from the roof of the car, but so far he hadn't figured out a way to get the flag up and attach it there. He might be able to poke a hole in the ceiling from inside and use the plumber's helper as a flagpole, but how would he ever get the square flag itself up on top of the outside of the wagon?

In the meantime the silver flag was outside the car and in a position to be seen. He went back to work with the lug wrench. First he jockeyed the tackle box down to the floor near the crushed glove compartment. Using it as a fulcrum, he placed the lug wrench across the tackle box and under the leading edge of the metal frame.

Closing his eyes, he said a short prayer: "Dear God, please make this work." He strained downward on the handle. The metal seemed to shift the tiniest fraction of an inch, but then, as he had feared, the lid of the tackle box cracked under the pressure. It simply wasn't strong enough. He needed a rock of some kind. At least he had learned that something strong enough to support the pressure of the wrench might work. But where to get that something was another matter.

Toward afternoon a sudden shower brought fresh worries. Jimmy was very close to the stream. A heavy rainfall followed by a flash flood could drown him. He took out his wallet and ripped a page off the book of receipts. On the front he wrote, "July 5," and on the back, "Worried about flash flood. Saw 9 cars and trucks. Chipmunks not around today. Made flag. Please, God, send someone fast."

He was tired of being scared all the time, he thought, as he lay back and tried to rest. Up to this point he had continued to hope that someone would notice the car lying in the bottom of the ravine and come down to check it out. That hope helped keep his fear under control. But as each day passed, the possibility of dying loomed more and more in his thoughts. There were too many things against him: He could die of hunger, thirst, exposure, flood, fire, blood poisoning. He could even die of sheer panic, he thought. And he didn't want to die—he had too many things to live for.

Animals, for one thing. If he couldn't become a vet, maybe he could open a special pet shop someday. Then he could take in all the wounded animals and birds and reptiles that people found in their yards and nurse them back to health and find good homes for them. Yeah, he knew what Dad would say: "It's not a very practical idea, now, is it, son?" For a moment he felt a flash of anger against his father and said aloud, "If you're so smart, Dad, how come you haven't found me yet?"

The sound of a car drew his attention, and he looked up at the road. He grabbed the wrench, but he was too late. A flash of chrome, a pulse of red from a taillight, and the car had passed. He dropped the wrench, then jerked on his leg. He had to get out! If something didn't happen soon, he'd go crazy.

All right, calm down, he told himself. *Think!* Somehow he had to get a rock into the front seat of the car. If he only had that bucket, maybe he could tumble a rock into it, then drag it back to the car. For the next hour he tried to snag the rim of the bucket with his fishing rod. Several times he managed to catch the hook under the lip, but the bucket was wedged between two rocks, and Jimmy was afraid of breaking his fishing rod. His only hope was that the constant pressure of the water against the side of the pail would finally cause it to shift position and pop free. Fortunately the bucket had nowhere to go, even if it came loose. The pool was encircled by a ring of stones and low boulders.

He heard another half-dozen vehicles pass on the road before darkness fell. Not one of them stopped or even slowed down. For supper he ate a quarter of a potato and several marshmallows, then finished up with some grass and leaves from outside the car. *Oh, for hotcakes and sausage,* he thought with a sigh, *and Mom's blueberry muffins, and fresh-squeezed orange juice, and bacon so crisp it practically stands to attention.* He groaned and took his hunger to bed with him.

That night he was awakened several times by the sound of rain drumming on the roof. Once he sat up and thought of fishing in the stream. If he had bait he could catch trout, if there were any trout in the stream. He grunted. It reminded him of one of Uncle Carl's sayings: "If we only had some bacon, we could have some bacon and eggs, if we only had some eggs." Still, fishing might be worth a try. Maybe he could use bits of marshmallow for bait. Why hadn't he thought of it before? First thing in the morning he would get to work on finding bait.

At 4:00 A.M. he awoke again, with the creepy feeling that someone or something was watching him. He heard movement in the bushes outside the car and then spotted the eyes, six of them! They were gleaming brightly in the darkness. For a moment he held his breath in fear. But he knew too much about animals to be truly frightened of them. As he once told Charlene, there was hardly a wild animal or bird or reptile in the world that wasn't more frightened of humans than we were of them, except maybe the grizzly bear, and the great white shark, and the elephant. At first he thought the eyes might belong to coyotes, but coyotes, he knew, rarely traveled together, though they might join in a pack to hunt deer.

The animals weren't more than a dozen yards away, just on the edge of the stream. As he grew accustomed to the dark, he recognized a white band around each eye.

"A family of raccoons," he said.

The raccoons must have stayed in the bushes, looking in at him, for a good ten minutes before they finally padded off and waded across the stream. He would have loved to have seen them in daylight, but they are mostly nocturnal animals, staying holed up asleep in their dens during the daytime.

He thought of Bandit, a raccoon he had half-tamed several years ago. One day he had spotted the black fur of some animal in a hole in a big rotted oak tree in the woods behind his house. The fur shifted position, and he found himself looking at yet another animal, a baby raccoon tightly gripping the belly of its mother. He took to visiting the raccoons and leaving walnuts and slices of bread for them at the foot of the tree. They grew quite used to him. Sometimes the mother, hanging upside down from the hole, the baby clinging to her fur, would contemplate him gravely as he talked to her. She seemed to have no fear of him at all. And then one day she and the baby were gone. Jimmy wondered if he had frightened her away, but later learned that it was common for raccoons to change nesting holes from time to time. He had never seen her or the baby again, and it surprised him how lonely he felt for a long time afterward, how much he missed them.

Jimmy fell asleep again toward dawn, wondering how much it would rain. Enough to flood the stream . . . ?

CHAPTER NINE

In the morning, after casting for a drink and cleaning his wound, Jimmy began to work on the problem of fishing and bait. He thought of using ants, since some had invaded the car, but they were too small. Grasshoppers were great trout bait, he knew, and every once in a while one went sailing by the window in a long hop, but his chances of catching one on the wing were practically zero.

He was left with either marshmallow or potato bits, and he didn't know which would work best. Finally he decided to put half a marshmallow on the hook.

On the second cast the bait fell into the pool. He propped the rod through the window frame, anchoring the end under the toolbox. He could always snatch it up if he saw the line jerking.

Every once in a while he would check the nylon line that trailed out from the end of the collapsible fishing rod. He probably wasn't going to catch anything. It was one of those bright ideas you got at 3:00 in the morning that just didn't stand up in daylight. For one thing, the marshmallow, which was almost pure sugar, would probably dissolve in the water.

Almost a week now, he thought, *a week at midnight.* And there wasn't nearly as much traffic today as there had been yesterday. Toward noon he did hear the sound of something approaching — something with a bad muffler, from the roar it was making. A minute passed, and he strained to get a glimpse of whatever was coming. Then the peculiar echoing sound of the exhaust told him, a second before he saw them, that two motorcycles were approaching! They were rolling down the grade, in the best position to get a look at the wrecked car in the canyon. He shouted and banged the car with the lug wrench. Surely the riders, with much better all-around vision than car drivers, would spot him. The bikers came slowly along, not trusting the loose gravel on the road. At one moment they seemed to slow almost to the point of stopping.

"Look down!" he shouted. "I'm down here! Hey, you guys, look down the slope!" Furiously he banged the lug wrench with all his might. "Help! Help! Help!" he screamed.

Then the bikes revved up and swept down the road and out of sight. Jimmy listened to the mufflers, praying that the noise would suddenly stop. The sound died to a murmur, ceased, murmured again as the bikes rounded another switchback, and then died away completely.

Jimmy lay back and groaned. It wasn't fair. They had practically stopped. Surely they must have seen something. What was the matter with them?

In anger and frustration he began jerking at his leg. "Come on, spring loose, damn you! I want out of here! Break if you have to!"

In minutes there were tears in his eyes, and finally he began to cry. It was all over. He knew it. He was going to die. There was just no way out. No one would ever find him.

Mercifully, the crying jag exhausted him and he fell asleep or passed out; he wasn't sure which. He must have slept for almost an hour before he woke up with sun streaming down into the interior of the car. He looked at his watch. It was almost 12:30. Had he missed any cars going by on the road? He grabbed the plumber's helper with the mirror and pushed it out the window, ready to signal. He twirled one end in his hand and aimed the other end toward the road. Why hadn't it been sunny when the motorcycles came along? It was funny, he hadn't thought of motorcyclists before, not until he had actually seen them coming.

What if a bicyclist came along on a camping trip or something? That wouldn't make any noise, and maybe the person would hear Jimmy banging and shouting in the ravine. But a rough gravel road was hardly the route a cyclist would take. How about ordinary hikers? Also unlikely. Hikers usually drove to a trailhead somewhere in the national forest, parked their cars, and headed off on foot. You hardly ever saw a hiker on a road like this.

Jimmy looked at the yellow bucket out in the pool. *If only the stream were big enough for white water canoeing,* he thought. And then, as long as he was working on "if onlys," if only he hadn't gone to the graduation night party at Hourglass Lake and met Susan who told him about Wayne coming home. If only he hadn't gotten mixed up with Charlene in the first place. If only he hadn't decided to drive to his Uncle Carl's place. If only he had left a note for Mom. If only he had worn his seat belt. If only someone would come rescue him. If only "if onlys" would work.

What did come along was an airplane, the second he had heard since the accident. It flew over so quickly that he never spotted it, though he could hear it plainly enough. It was probably a forest service patrol plane, spot-checking for fires. Or was it possible they were searching for him? He doubted it. It wasn't as though he were in a downed plane, or something like that. No one knew he had gone off the road in the station wagon. He bet most people thought he had run off to Alaska or California. Eighteen-year-old kids were constantly taking off for far away places, especially after graduation.

He lifted the end of the fishing rod and reeled in to see how his marshmallow looked. Most of the candy had melted away. Only a tiny white smear was left.

He took out the receipts, tore off a page, and filled in the date, July 6. On the back, he wrote, "Sunday. 7th day stuck here. Fishing won't work. 2 bikes and 1 plane passed. Feel rotten."

Then, for want of something better to do, he picked up the lug wrench and tried again to lever the crumpled metal away from his foot. Hopeless. He waved the end of the wrench around underneath the dashboard on the driver's side and managed to hook a group of wires. He pulled at them until they were within reach, then jerked them free. The electrical lines were sheathed within a black plastic tube. Jimmy worked all the wires free. He tossed the protective tube aside. He now had eight lengths of thin copper wire, each approximately two feet long. If he replaced the nylon line on his fishing rod with copper wire, maybe it would be strong enough to retrieve the bucket. He reached behind him and found one of the thin aluminum header strips he had taken off earlier to get to the ceiling liner. Suddenly he had an even better idea. If he could make a little hook at one end of the strip, then tie the other end to the top of the fishing rod, the aluminum would surely be strong enough to lift the bucket out. With a pair of pliers, he formed a small hook at one end of the strip and lined up the other end with the tip of the fishing rod so that both objects overlapped about a foot. Then he tightly wrapped the overlap with copper wire to make sure it would hold. He eased his contraption out the window and found that the hook just barely reached as far as the bucket. Working the hook under the lip, he pulled carefully on the fishing rod. Would the overlap hold the weight?

The bucket popped right up, and Jimmy let out a shout. Soon he had it within reach. An inch of water was in the bottom, and he drank it gratefully. He didn't know why, but recovering the bucket gave a tremendous lift to his spirits. One of his wild ideas had actually panned out. He found himself talking to his dad, imagining some future explanation he would make: "You see, Dad, I made a little hook on the end of the aluminum strip. And then I tied it to the . . ." He laughed at himself. That was hardly likely to impress his dad.

Now for another wild idea — unwrap the wire, take off the header strip, attach the bucket to the rod, and push it back out there to see if he could maneuver a rock into it. He just hoped he wouldn't lose the bucket again. He lowered the rod tip, and the bucket dropped down beside a stone. He bounced the bucket up and down until it fell on its side. With his other hand, he pushed the aluminum strip out the window and nudged the stone inside the bucket.

"So far so good," he muttered. But would the combined weight of the stone and bucket be too much for the line? Keeping the rod tip down, he reeled in slowly, and the bucket slid and skidded over the ground until it was just outside the window. He had done it! With shaking hands, Jimmy brought the stone into the car.

The stone was about the size and shape of a large orange, and he let it roll down his legs until it hit the floor. Then he nudged it into position, rested one end of the lug wrench on top of it, and used it as a fulcrum. He pushed down on the wrench. Now he was going to free himself. But again, because he couldn't sit up, he was unable to press down on the end of the lug wrench with the full weight of his shoulders. Anyway, the other end of the wrench kept sliding off the rounded surface of the rock. Again and again Jimmy reset the tool, and again and again it slid off. After a dozen attempts he gave up. He would need a much larger stone, one that wasn't so round, something the size and shape of a loaf of bread, perhaps. But how would he ever get such a stone over to the car? It would be too heavy for the fishing rod.

He laid the lug wrench aside and rested for a moment. Outside the window Flash and Trigger appeared, racing here and there through the underbrush, stopping periodically to rise up on their hind legs and chatter in to him.

"Okay, you guys," he greeted them. "You want more marshmallows, right? I can't keep feeding you, you know. You ought to be bringing me food."

Flash raced forward, stopped, and sat up on his hind legs.

Despite his grim position, Jimmy felt a sense of achievement. He had gotten his bucket back, hadn't he? He had figured out a way to get small rocks from the stream and over to the car. He had made a signal mirror and a flag to attract attention, right? All in all, not bad for a klutz.

For some reason he began to shiver. The fit lasted a full minute, then stopped as suddenly as it started. Was he coming down with a cold? he wondered. Thank God, the weather had been mild so far. The worst night couldn't have been any cooler than sixty degrees. But maybe the lack of adequate food was beginning to lower his resistance.

To conserve strength, he decided to take another nap. After an hour or so, during which he hardly slept more than five minutes at a stretch, he still felt weak and also somewhat nauseous. Perhaps the water in the bucket hadn't been very clean, although it had certainly looked all right. And now, to make matters worse, the sun was hidden again, the clouds growing thicker and heavier. It looked as though a storm was on the way.

For the rest of Sunday, his seventh day of captivity, Jimmy lay in the car, counting the cars that went by on the road. By the time darkness fell, he had made eleven pencil marks on a piece of ceiling liner.

CHAPTER TEN

Sometime during the night it began to rain heavily, and Jimmy woke up on Monday morning to gray skies and a steady downpour. Water was coursing down the drip gutter of the roof, and he had merely to stick his bucket outside for a moment to have all he wanted to drink. He took his morning drink, ate two marshmallows and half a potato, then looked around the inside of the wagon for leaks. Water was dripping steadily through a crease in the metal roof. It suddenly occurred to him that he could make a hole in the ceiling. He could make another kind of signal by sticking something through the roof of the car, since he had not been able to fly his flag.

Working patiently, he made a hole in the roof by hammering the screwdriver through it, then fed one end of an aluminum strip up through the hole until two feet or so was sticking above roof-level. The strip fitted snugly. He hoped it would attract attention. With the cloudy weather, the mirror and the aluminum flag were useless.

All morning only two cars passed, and neither of them slowed down. He filled another entry in his diary. "Monday. Steady rain. Made hole in roof. Light traffic." After that he unwound the bandage from his arm to look at the wound. No more bits of glass appeared, and the cut seemed to be healing normally. It didn't seem as deep as it had at first, which meant the tissues were coming together. And so far it wasn't infected, although the skin was somewhat red and swollen. He washed it with the liner rag and rolled down his sleeve.

Early in the afternoon he noticed that the stream was rising. The pool closest to his car had spread, and tiny bits of debris were showing up in the water, small branches and occasional clumps of brush. If the stream got much higher, he thought, the water would come within reach of his arm, and he could dip it up with the bucket. On the other hand, if the stream got too high, then water would enter the car and soak him to the skin. It could even drown him, although he didn't think there was much chance of that happening. The only problem was that the warm weather and the heavy rain might melt the snows too quickly up in the high mountains, causing a swift runoff that would turn the stream into a torrent. If that happened he was doomed, no question about it. He wouldn't stand a hope of surviving a flood. He shivered. *Don't even think about it,* he told himself.

Some time later, a crashing noise downstream startled him, causing a great leap in his spirits.

Was someone coming? He sat up as best he could and looked out through the open windshield. For minutes he saw nothing, then a dark blur among some young pines caught his attention. What was it, a deer? A bear! He could clearly make out the animal now. It was about a hundred yards downstream, turning over a dead log, grubbing for beetles underneath. He watched the bear and thought how clumsy it looked and yet how gracefully it moved. The animal ambled off and seemed to melt away among the trees as though it were a shadow.

Jimmy lay back again and closed his eyes. *How could anyone shoot such marvelous animals?* he wondered. That was another argument between him and his dad. His dad loved to hunt, but Jimmy could no longer bear the thought of killing anything, especially something as beautiful as a deer or a bear. But to his dad, hunting was the sign of a man. If you were a man, you got your gun and went off in the woods and tracked down some animal and knocked it off. Big deal. Once he had argued with Charlene about it. He explained to her how he felt about hunting, how it was always easy to kill something but a whole lot harder to keep it alive. He told her he wouldn't even kill a rattlesnake.

"Not even if I asked you to?" she said.

"Not even then," he answered. "Unless it was about to strike you or something like that."

"But you killed a rattlesnake once, you even showed me the rattle," she said.

"I was just a kid and didn't know any better," he answered.

It was true. He used to kill snakes and mice and frogs. But that was before the time he shot the finch. A couple of years ago Andy had gotten a new BB gun for his birthday and was out in the yard, banging away at things, when Jimmy borrowed the gun and aimed at a finch on a branch, not really expecting to hit it.

He pressed the trigger and was astonished to see the bird fall to the ground. He and Andy ran over. The finch was flopping around on the grass. He picked it up and its tiny head fell to one side. He straightened the head and it flopped again. There was no sign of the pellet. He had obviously broken the bird's neck. The eyes were still open, and the beak would silently gape wide, then close again. Through all of this the wings were flapping slightly as the bird tried to fly. He could actually feel its heart beating under the feathers. Jimmy had felt terrible, and it was an hour or more before the bird finally died. After that he swore he would never kill another living thing, and so far he hadn't.

The discussion with Charlene about hunting had finally turned into an argument. She fiercely defended the rights of hunters to go out and shoot any animal they wanted. It was even in the Constitution, she claimed. What was funny was that no one in her family hunted. Her dad worked as manager of the meat counter in the supermarket, and he used to joke that he saw enough dead animals in his work without going out looking for more on his days off. Then it suddenly dawned on Jimmy. Wayne hunted. He liked to go gunning for ducks during the fall. He probably went deer hunting, too. He'd really been blind when it came to Charlene.

Drowsily, Jimmy became aware of a slight snuffling noise that seemed to be part of the murmuring background sound of running water. Then a loud grunt came from just outside the car. Jimmy jerked wide-awake.

A large brown bear was staring in at him! The animal stood up and placed its shaggy front paw on top of the station wagon's hood. For a moment Jimmy panicked and grabbed for his knife. Then reason took hold of him, and he tried to calm down. What harm could the bear do? He doubted it could get inside the car. So far there was no sign that it even wanted to.

He looked at the bear, realizing he had never seen one so close before. Its fur was dark and gleaming with pearls of rain. After another inquisitive growl, it dropped to all fours again, its head resting in the frame of the front window on the driver's side. Suddenly it thrust its black button of a nose inside the window, sniffing around, the lips drawn back in a grin, showing huge yellow teeth. Jimmy shrank back. The bear could easily tear his arm or leg off with one of those paws if it wanted to. He thought briefly of throwing it a marshmallow but decided against it. Bears loved sweet things, and feeding it might make it want more. Moving cautiously,

Jimmy reached back and drew his sleeping bag over the food bag.

Now the bear's head was to one side, pressing against the frame of the window, while one paw reached inside. Jimmy held his breath. There was absolutely nothing he could do. If he shouted or tried to hit it, he would only anger it and make things worse. You were supposed to play dead if you were ever trapped by a bear. And that's what he tried to do — stay as still as he possibly could, breathing with controlled, shallow breaths. He shut his eyes, determined not to open them until the bear's next move.

Suddenly the bear withdrew and went galumphing off through the bushes, and Jimmy called softly after it, "Good-bye." And then — he could not explain why — he found himself crying. It was partly with relief and partly with a tremendous feeling of gratitude that he had been given those several moments with the bear.

He shivered and then realized he was sweating. He wiped his brow. It was close inside the car, especially with the humid weather, but he knew that the sweat came also from the tension he had been under the past few minutes. He ached with loneliness. In the meantime it was still raining, and just before darkness fell, he was startled to see how much the stream had risen.

He laid his head back on the sleeping bag and thought of the bear. It was almost as though Jimmy were an animal in some zoo, at whose cage the bear had stopped for a moment. He gave a short laugh. Somehow he felt that the bear—was a sign to him, a test he had passed, and that he was going to survive his ordeal. The animal's visit hadn't changed a thing, but in a curious way he felt that the worst was over.

It wasn't.

CHAPTER ELEVEN

During the night Jimmy woke up every half hour or so. The erratic beating of the rain on the metal roof made it difficult to stay asleep, and the car was leaking in several places. Water seemed to be getting in everywhere, around the edges of the badly sprung doors, through the open windshield and broken side windows. Worried about his food spoiling, he wrapped it in aluminum foil and bundled it away in the foot of the sleeping bag.

When dawn came he found that the water in the stream had risen considerably and was now only a few feet away. If it rose much higher, it would start seeping into the car itself.

After a breakfast of two marshmallows and a quarter of a potato, he decided to try to work a larger rock from the stream into the car. He had noticed one that just might be big enough for his purpose. It was about the size and shape of a lunchbox, though not as rounded on top. He used the header strip of aluminum with the hook at one end to nudge the rock toward him.

After what seemed like hours, he had maneuvered it to the side of the car and was able to walk it partway up the car door. Twice it fell back to the ground, but on his third attempt he managed to get it high enough to grab and lift into the car.

Jimmy lowered the rock into place near the metal collar, moving it around and, with his left foot, positioning it exactly where he wanted it. He closed his eyes and remained motionless for a couple of minutes to rest his arms, needing all his strength for the next move. He took a deep breath and carefully inserted the sharp end of the lug wrench between the rock and the crumpled piece of metal holding his foot. Pushing down as hard as he could, he rolled his body onto the bar to get more leverage. A creaking, metallic noise caused his heart to race. Was it giving? He tugged his left foot. Still trapped! Gritting his teeth, he tried again. Even with the extra pressure, he was unable to lift the piece of metal enough to free his foot. Panting from his efforts, he rested a moment, then turned the rock over on its side so that it sat on edge. That way he might get more leverage on it. Once again he rolled over on the handle and once again failed. After trying several different positions, he was forced to give up. It just wouldn't work.

For the thousandth time he went over his desperate situation. His foot was trapped. *Think!* he scolded himself. *Okay, so you're no good with your hands, but you don't have to build a cathedral or anything like that. All you have to do is get your foot free. Think!* Okay, he could cut his foot off — that would certainly free him. *Sure, cut your foot off — brilliant idea.* So that left the metal itself. What could he do to metal? Melt it, but he had no torch. Saw it with a hacksaw, but he had no blade. What else could you do with metal but saw it and burn it? Wear it away. But with what? Blast it with a laser gun. Yeah, *Star Wars* stuff. Nothing else.

He covered his face with both hands and groaned. *Give up,* he told himself, *you're going to die.* What day was it, Tuesday? Tuesday, July 8th. How many days was it now? Sunday night was a week, Monday, Tuesday — his ninth day. How much longer could he last? He reached into the foot of his sleeping bag and came up with the marshmallows and half a potato. He could finish the potato and marshmallows today. How many more days could he go without food — four or five? Taking out his knife, he cut a thin slice off one end of the potato and popped it in his mouth, then put everything away again. Slowly savoring each shred, he chewed on the potato until it was all gone.

"Mom!" he called aloud. "I want a big dish of spaghetti, just the way you make it, with a sauce of garlic, parsley, olive oil, walnuts, and oregano. And a loaf of Italian bread, fresh from the oven, steaming hot." *And fresh peaches,* he thought. What he wouldn't give for a fresh peach right now. And a tossed salad. A salad!

He reached his arm out the front window and

felt around on the ground, trying to locate some grass, leaves, a piece of shrub, anything. He finally managed to find a twig that he broke in half and began to chew. Was there any food value in a twig? He chewed both halves until they were a sodden mass of fibers, then spat them out. With the hook end of his aluminum strip he foraged through the nearby bushes, trying to strip off some leaves. He managed to pull in a spray of leaves, and he picked off half a dozen and ate them. They had a slightly bitter taste, but he forced them down. Maybe they had some food value. He had better enjoy them because in another day or two, by the look of things, he'd be eating dirt.

With his liner rag he caught water dripping from the roof and washed his hands and face, his neck, and as much of his upper body as he could reach. He also brushed his teeth with a corner of the rag. It was a pity he had lost his toilet kit; he could have used the soap. He could even have eaten the toothpaste. Maybe the rising stream would bring a dead animal along. Oh, sure and maybe a McDonald's would come floating by. Or a Kentucky Fried Chicken. *Quit thinking about food,* he told himself. *Think about getting out.* But instead he thought about death. His own death.

Would Charlene go to his funeral? he wondered. Probably not. She had been so warm toward him. Then suddenly, *bang!* Overnight, she had changed. At first she had been very loving. Once, in this very station wagon with her arms around him, she had said, "It's *you* I love." *And not Wayne*, Jimmy had thought. It was as though she were trying to convince herself. *Forget her, stop thinking about her*, he wanted to shout.

Then he heard a chittering in the underbrush and caught sight of a tiny furry body disappearing into a cleft between two rocks. "Flash! Trigger!" he called. The wet weather was keeping them in their ground holes, he realized. He missed them.

He heard the sound of a car in the distance. Grabbing the lug wrench, he began to beat on the ceiling. "Help!" he shouted. "*Help!*"

Even as he banged on the metal, half-deafening himself, he was aware that he was making all that noise not so much to be heard as to drown out the sound of the car passing by. He couldn't bear the thought of rescue being so close and yet almost impossible.

Jimmy stopped shouting. He could hear the car no longer. Throwing the wrench down, he pulled the sleeping bag up over his shoulders. Whatever was going to happen, he thought, he sure wished it would happen soon, whether he was going to drown, or die of starvation, or what. One thing for sure, he would never complain about being bored again ever in his whole life, because this was the most boring time he had ever spent, the most boring place he had ever been in, even more boring than Boise, Idaho, as Mom liked to say.

Just before it grew dark, he noticed that the water level had risen at least another six inches.

If the stream kept flooding at the same rate, water would be inside the car by morning. And if the rain kept up, he would get little sleep that night, either. And yet he ached with exhaustion, right through to the very marrow of his bones.

Chapter Twelve

Jimmy woke up at 5:00 on Wednesday morning with a burning pain in his arm. As soon as there was enough light, he unrolled the sleeve and took off the bandage. One end of the cut was infected, the flesh around the wound angry and swollen. Already pus was forming, and he wondered whether some glass was still in there.

He dug out the washing cloth, which he was careful to keep separate from the drinking cloth, and dipped it in the water that was now within arm's reach of the window. Gritting his teeth against the pain, he washed the red and swollen tissues, holding the rag on the infected part for a long time. Then he washed out the rag and repeated the process. After a dozen soakings he thought he had drawn most of the pus out. He probed at the wound with his knife, feeling for tiny bits of glass. The pain was so intense that his eyes watered. He didn't locate any more glass, and finally he wrapped his arm again and rolled down the sleeve of his shirt.

It had been raining steadily now for twenty-four hours. The stream level was much higher. Jimmy dipped his drinking rag in the water outside the window and took several swallows. Then he ate two slices of potato and three marshmallows. He had six marshmallows and less than a quarter of a potato left. The lack of food was beginning to tell on him, though oddly enough he still didn't feel very hungry, not beyond a dull stomachache that periodically came and went. But he did feel a lot more tired than he used to. It seemed to take great effort just to roll over on one hip when he wanted to reach for something. It was bad enough to feel clumsy, but worse to feel weak on top of that.

He looked again at the metal bracket neatly trapping his ankle. He had tried to pry away the legs of the arch, but that hadn't worked. What else could he do? Supposing he were to cut through the high point of the arch and separate the metal at what was probably its weakest point. Couldn't he then push away one of the legs? It might work. The light steel frame of the glove compartment didn't look all that strong. But what could he cut the metal with? How about a chisel? You could cut wood with a chisel, but could you cut metal?

He had a vague memory of his dad cutting a piece of heavy steel wire with a chisel. In his mind's eye he could see him carefully placing the cutting edge of the chisel on top of the steel strands. Half a dozen quick, precise blows of the hammer against the chisel and the wire was neatly cut through. But he didn't have a chisel.

And even if he had a chisel, he didn't have a hammer.

Groaning, he rolled over on one hip and looked out at the stream. The water level was still rising and had gained another couple of inches since daybreak. After ten minutes, he rolled over on his back again. His foil flag, he noticed, had disappeared, carried off by the stream. Rain was dripping down from the spot where his header strip stuck up through the hole in the roof. He had a quick image of himself making that hole, pounding on the handle of the screwdriver to force the point up through the crease in the metal. Wait a minute, he had a hammer! That small round rock, where was it? Maybe with a screwdriver he could still work something out.

He found the toolbox, opened it, and went through the screwdrivers. They were all too light to use as a chisel. The lug wrench! Maybe that would do. He picked up the tool and examined it again. The screwdriver end was about half an inch wide, and the other end would surely be strong enough to take hammer blows. And it was just about long enough, too. The big problem was that the screwdriver end was too blunt to cut anything. It was somewhat squared off, instead of being sharp like the edge of a chisel. Maybe he could sharpen it. For that he would need a file, or a grinding wheel . . . or a rock. And he had two.

He patted around with his hand and came up with the smaller rock. Would it really work as a sharpening stone? Jamming one end of the lug wrench under his thigh, he went to work and began running the round stone over the narrow end of the tool. He stroked it fifty times, turned it over, then did fifty more. After a hundred strokes, he held up the wrench. The edge didn't seem any sharper, though he could see the bright, polished patch where the stone had been wearing away at the metal. He did one hundred more strokes. It was tiring work, but over the next hour he actually did more than a thousand strokes and was finally rewarded to see a definite sharpening of the tip of the wrench. He was actually shaping an edge! But the work was taking its toll on him. It was exhausting, especially with the pain from the infected wound. He could no longer do fifty strokes at a time, only ten or so before he was forced to stop for a rest. But he kept at it until the pain was too much and he simply had to quit for a while. He checked his watch. *Quarter of an hour's rest,* he told himself — then he would get back to work.

During the rest of the afternoon, while he worked on the lug wrench in fits and starts, half a dozen cars passed by. Just before the last of the evening light drained from the sky, he noticed that the water level had continued to rise and would soon enter the car.

He had to get out before that happened. He was in a race with time. He snatched up the rock and went back to work on the lug wrench, grinding away as much as his aching muscles would allow. Finally darkness, pain, and misery put an end to his efforts.

Lying back, he wondered just how the end would come if the car flooded. He would keep his head raised as high as he could, he supposed, until finally the water reached his chin. Then he would tilt his head back, trying to keep his face level, until the water, still rising, would enter his nostrils, and then it would be all over. He shivered. What an awful way to die! Surely that couldn't happen to Jimmy Korne, could it?

That night he was afraid to go to sleep. Every ten minutes or so he woke up and patted the floor beneath him, feeling for water. An hour before daybreak, he realized that his feet were wet and knew the stream had now entered the station wagon. Could he get that piece of metal cut before the rising water made it impossible to work on it anymore?

He grabbed the lug wrench and small grinding stone.

Chapter Thirteen

By early the next morning the water was several inches deep in the station wagon. Actually, the rain had eased off somewhat, giving Jimmy the hope that the stream would soon crest and start to go down again. But he couldn't count on that, he knew. He had to prepare for the worst and assume that the water would rise another foot, or maybe two.

After cleaning out his wound, which was still infected, he washed his hands and face and ate two slices of potato and one marshmallow. He had just enough food for one more skimpy meal. He wondered how much weight he had lost. At least ten pounds, he thought, if he went by the fact that his belt was now two notches tighter.

Listlessly he took up the lug wrench and went back to sharpening the edge. For some reason his enthusiasm of yesterday had melted away. His efforts swiftly ate away his last reserves of strength. He was forced to rest after every half-dozen strokes or so. His forearms, wrists, hands, even his fingers, were numb with fatigue and cramping with pain. Anyway, the whole idea was too complicated to work.

By noon the water had risen another foot, and he worried about losing his few possessions. With the copper wires he had earlier ripped out from under the dashboard, he tied all his things together. He ran wire through the handles of the tool and tackle boxes, and through one end of the bucket and into the tie strings of his sleeping bag. With everything tied together, he attached it to the post of a seat belt so that none of the stuff could float off through the open windshield. That took him at least an hour and he was exhausted. Just when he thought he was through, he came across the long tube of black plastic that had formed the protective cover around the copper wires. He was putting it away in the tackle box when an image popped his mind: an Indian, underwater, breathing through a reed.

He had once read about an Indian brave who jumped into a stream to avoid his enemies. The Indian lay on the streambed and breathed through a long reed, one end of which stuck up above the surface of the water. When his enemies got tired of searching for him and left, the Indian crawled out of the stream and went on his way. Why couldn't Jimmy do what the Indian did . . . if he had to?

He pulled the aluminum strip out of the hole in the roof and pushed the end of the tube up through it. It stuck above the surface of the roof a foot or more. He raised his head to the lower end of the tube and caught it between his teeth.

He sucked air through the opening, released his breath through his nostrils, breathed in again, breathed out. It seemed to work. Of course, he didn't know what it would be like to use the tube underwater. If the breathing end slipped out of his mouth, he would have only a minute or so to find it again. He put the tube safely away in his shirt.

He went back to sharpening the edge of his lug wrench. He did five strokes with the stone, rested for a count of ten, then did five more strokes. He seemed to be working on it forever, but by early afternoon he actually had a sharp enough edge to test his makeshift chisel. He set the edge against the high point of the metal arch and held the other end steady with his left hand. Then he gave it a good whack with the stone. He could feel the end of the wrench biting into the metal. He lowered the tool to take a look. There was a definite impression. It wasn't deep, to be sure, but it was there, a slight nick. He tried another blow, then a third, and looked again.

"All right!" he shouted. He was actually cutting the metal! A dozen whacks later, he lowered the wrench and checked the cut again. For some reason his chisel wasn't cutting anymore, at least not the way it had at first. He pulled the lug wrench back and looked at the cutting end. He would have to sharpen it again. Despite his aching arms, he picked up the stone and began grinding away. Half an hour later, he renewed his attack on the piece of metal. But he was now very tired, his blows weak and unsteady. Once the cutting edge skidded off the metal and gouged a piece of flesh out of his ankle. He screamed with pain. He suspected the ankle was bleeding, but he couldn't tell as his foot was underwater. Despite the pain and his aching muscles, he grimly went back to sharpening and hammering. Once again the edge was dulled and he was forced to stop.

The water had risen above his foot to within an inch or two of the metal he was trying to cut. He worked feverishly now, trying to resharpen the edge, but the harder he worked, the more tired he became and the more mistakes he made. Finally the water reached the metal frame itself and he had to give up. Both feet were now underwater.

The stream was flowing with a lot more force now, carrying along with it clumps of debris. Occasionally an uprooted tree would smash into the back of the station wagon.

Once he heard a truck passing by on the road, and although he had given up any hope of rescue from that direction, he still went through the motions of banging on the roof with the lug wrench.

Another floating log smacked into the back of the wagon, and the whole vehicle tilted up a couple of inches. Jimmy yelled in fright, thinking that the car was going over on its side, but it settled down again.

He wondered about Flash and Trigger. He hadn't seen hide nor hair of them all day. They had probably scampered to higher ground. He missed them. The only living thing he had seen that day had been a small snake on the far bank of the stream. He had glimpsed a bright green coil straightening out, followed by a wriggling movement underneath some leaves. He wondered about snakes in the stream, caught by the rising floodwater. Uncle Carl told him of once seeing a dozen rattlesnakes curled around the roots of an old dead tree floating down a river in a flood. The snakes must have had a den under the tree, Carl had said, and when it toppled into the river, it carried a dozen of the snakes along with it, coiled in the roots. He shivered. *Just don't let any rattlers come floating into the car*, he prayed. He had troubles enough.

Again and again during the night, the car was struck by branches and debris, which meant that he couldn't get much sleep. Anyway, he was too cold, and the rushing water was very noisy. Jimmy worried about the plastic tube that he had stashed inside his shirt. At first he thought of sticking it up through the hole in the roof and leaving it there, but he was afraid it might somehow be carried away. He had to have that tube — it was his lifeline. He was so afraid of losing it that he changed its hiding place several times. And indeed once he did lose it when he forgot the latest hiding place and had to search, panic-stricken, for a good five minutes before he found it again.

All night he wondered if he would be forced to use the tube before daylight came. He knew the water was still rising. He could feel it at his chest. He would not like to have to thread the piece of black tubing through the hole while it was still dark.

This was by far his worst night, Jimmy realized. He was absolutely exhausted, and yet he could not, dared not, sleep. To keep his sanity he began making mental lists. He had read somewhere of a prisoner who walked a set number of steps every day in his cell. He figured so many steps to a mile, and then how many miles it was to the nearest town, how many miles from that town to Paris, how many miles from Paris to New York. The prisoner had a map of the world in his cell, and using a thumbtack, he kept track of his imaginary trip on the map. When he was released seven years later, he had walked almost completely around the world.

Jimmy couldn't walk around the world, but to keep his mind from dwelling on the horrors of his own imprisonment, he began making up lists: a list of all the kids in his class, a list of all the different mammals he had ever seen, a list of all his relatives, and a list of all the states he had ever been in — only five. He made a list of all the pets he had owned at one time or another and came up with twenty-three.

Then he imagined he was a prisoner condemned to death. What did he want for his last meal? He planned it carefully, changing his order a dozen times, finally deciding that if he ever found himself in that fix, he would order five thousand artichokes for his last meal. Nothing took longer to eat than an artichoke, he figured.

Through it all, his imagination kept playing tricks on him. At times he was sure the water level was falling. At other times he was positive it was rising. He had a feeling that the rain had stopped, but it was difficult to tell with the raging waters creating so much splash and drizzle.

He yearned desperately for dawn to come and was just as desperately afraid of what daylight would reveal.

Chapter Fourteen

An hour before dawn, Jimmy could see through the windshield opening a strip of black sky dotted with a dozen tiny pinpricks of starlight. It had stopped raining. When the first gray light appeared in the canyon and he was able to check the flood, he found that the water level was still rising. He was disappointed but not surprised. He could only pray that the flood would soon reach its crest and level off.

He raised his left arm out of the water to check the time and found that his watch had stopped. Now underwater up to the middle of his shoulders, he worried about keeping his head high enough. He placed the tool and tackle boxes on top of each other, then rested the back of his head on the makeshift platform. Now he was halfway comfortable and did not have to strain to keep his nose and mouth out of the water.

Later that morning, the water having gained another couple of inches, Jimmy looked out and saw Flash and Trigger racing madly back and forth on the bank above him. He wondered what was wrong with them. Perhaps their underground nest had flooded out. Did they have any young to look after? If so, they had probably moved them to a safer location. Animals had an instinct about things like that.

He had a kink in his neck from resting it on the boxes, and tried to move into a more comfortable position, but his head slipped off the topmost box and went under water. At the same time a large branch banged into the back of the wagon. The car was turning over! He would drown! But Jimmy managed to strain his head up, his face close to the ceiling. He had to do something — and fast!

He reached inside his shirt and felt for the tube of plastic. Fishing it out, he worked one end up and through the hole in the ceiling. He pushed until most of the tube was sticking above the roof of the car. Then he raised his head and put the other end of the plastic tube into his mouth. He breathed in and out a couple of times to make sure nothing was blocking the passage of air. He took one last look around and lowered his head underwater. For a few seconds fear again clutched at him as the first breath he drew pulled water into his mouth. He clamped his right hand over his face, leaving room for the tube between his middle fingers. There, that was better. He drew in a long, deep breath, inhaled no water, and blew out again through his nose. He could feel the air bubbles brushing his forehead. Soon he had a regular rhythm of breathing worked out. He began counting breaths. He would stay under for at least a hundred breaths. At the end of the hundred, he raised his head out of the water and looked around. The water level was now within six inches of the ceiling. There was still enough space left so that he could put the tube away again for a while. At least he had proved that he could breathe with his whole head underwater. Which meant, counting the foot or more of the tube above the roof and the six inches still left in the interior of the car, that he had almost two feet of breathing room left. And now that the rain had stopped, surely the flood would slacken before he ran out of space.

Flash and Trigger had disappeared, he noticed. He just hoped they had found a new nest somewhere, well above the flood line.

He wondered what his family was going through at home. Some people would think he had run away, gone off to San Francisco, or L.A., or New York. What else could they think when not even his car was found? He was a missing person. The police departments in those cities might have his picture on file by now. Or did they bother once you were eighteen? Well, practically eighteen, in another day or two. But surely Mom and Dad wouldn't think he had run off. They knew him too well. Perhaps they were searching all the ravines on all the roads along which he might have driven. Of course, Dad would get others to help him look, his fire department buddies, the guys he worked with, the men on his bowling team.

What day was it? He had lost track. Was it Friday the 11th? Or Saturday the 12th? The 13th was his birthday. The days had started to run into one another, especially since he had not been able to write in his diary. The pages were all wet. He should have tried to keep his wallet dry. It was too late now, though.

As the day wore on, the water level continued to rise. It was over two days since he had gotten any real sleep. His head would droop, his eyes close, but then the fear of going under would jerk him wide-awake again. Anyway, the car was being constantly nudged and bumped by floating debris. At least he wasn't facing upstream. With the windshield broken out, all kinds of junk would come floating inside.

Despite himself, he closed his eyes late in the afternoon and drifted into a half-conscious, half-daydreaming state, still very much aware of the water slopping against his neck. Dying couldn't be that bad, he thought. It was probably like going to the dentist, a lot worse in your imagination than in real life. He would just quietly pass out; there would be no pain, just a great peace. He could feel that peace settle over him as he took final leave of his body and became a scarf of mist that trailed out the window. The mist gathered into a loose puffball, and Jimmy floated higher and higher over the canyon. Down below he could see the station wagon and the dark shadow that was his own body. He could see the road and an oil truck laboring up the grade. He rose higher and higher. Somewhere above him was a great brilliance. And then he saw them: a crowd of people standing in an open meadow, bathed by intense rays of white light. There was his Grandad Ross, who had died four years ago, and the Sweeney twins and Eleanor Field and Uncle Carl's wife, Aunt Clara, and Mrs. Quincey, the school crossing guard. They were all old friends and would welcome him. But as he floated closer he could see that they were waving him back, saying, "No, no, not yet!"

But he wanted to be with them, and he strained forward. In an instant everyone disappeared, and Jimmy found himself in the backyard at home, playing with Flash. He was called into the house then and Mom yelled at him for leaving the back door open and letting all the flies in. He sat down at the kitchen table, where Mom was setting out a bowl of soup. Mysteriously, he was sitting in a high chair. He was only two years old. Neither Andy nor Candy were around; they hadn't been born yet, and Jimmy felt sly because he knew this and his folks didn't.

He wasn't going to tell them, either, at least not yet.

Then Dad came in from a job and set his folding rule on the table. From his high chair, Jimmy reached out and began to play with it. The sections would slide out, and then slide out some more. It was wonderful the way the rule kept getting longer and longer.

"Be careful," his father said. "Don't break it."

He opened the rule still further and made a fence with it, a series of X's, just like his playpen in the living room. Then he tried to make one of the sections go against the hinge, and it suddenly snapped off. He stared at the broken piece in his hand.

"Now you've done it!" his dad shouted. "I told you to watch it!" He snatched up both parts of the rule. "I've had this rule for six years!" he shouted.

"For heaven's sakes, he's only a child," Mom said.

"He shouldn't have touched it!" his dad shouted. He stood up, and a huge red face towered over Jimmy. He shrank back in his high chair.

"Don't ever touch any of my tools again, do you hear? You're a clumsy klutz!"

That terrifying face kept getting closer and closer.

"No!" Jimmy cried out. "No . . . no . . ."

He woke up spluttering, half-expecting to see

his dad beside him. He had fallen asleep, and his head had gone under. Spitting water out of his mouth, he wiped strands of dank hair out of his eyes. What a weird dream. Or was it a childhood memory? Vaguely he recalled something about a broken rule. Could he remember back that far? He would have to ask Dad about it.

For as long as he could remember he had never touched any of his father's tools. Even now he asked permission when he wanted to use a wrench or screwdriver. Andy just took what he wanted. Maybe he wasn't clumsy at all. Maybe he just *thought* he was clumsy.

Jimmy shivered and looked around. The water level inside the car didn't seem to be rising anymore. Suddenly he was aware of a sharp pain in his trapped ankle. Something must have struck it when he went under. Either that or he had kicked it with his free foot. He was a mess all right — cold, wet, sick, miserable, and in pain — but at least he was still alive.

Several hours later, the water level inside the car had actually declined an inch or so. It continued to drop, and by nightfall he could raise his arm completely free of the water. The cut still hurt him, and he wanted to unroll the bandage and look at it, but everything was sopping wet. Having hung on this long, he could wait until morning. Then he could take off the shirt and wash everything out and perhaps even dry the bandage and shirt in the sun.

Sometime shortly before dawn Jimmy fell sound asleep. Once his head rolled off the boxes, but it fell onto the wet sleeping bag, now well clear of the water.

He didn't even wake up.

CHAPTER FIFTEEN

The next morning the water was completely gone from the car. The stream was still high, but the flood was over and Jimmy knew it was zero day. If he didn't succeed in cutting himself free before nightfall, he would die right there in the car.

It seemed to take forever to get the lug wrench out. It was jammed under the front seat, and he had trouble pulling it free.

A flash of motion outside the window drew his attention, and there were the chipmunks, racing around on the bank outside the window. They were chattering to him again.

"Okay, fellows, I'll get busy, but I don't think it's going to work," he told them.

The chipmunks kept up their scolding. Unfortunately he had no marshmallows left to feed them. Reluctantly he went back to tugging at the lug wrench and finally succeeded in yanking it free.

He sat up as much as he could and placed the end of the lug wrench against the top of the metal arch. He struck a blow. It was a pitifully weak effort. He would have to do much better than that. He replaced the wrench and this time swung with all his might. The stone glanced sideways off the end of the wrench and flew out of his hand to land on the floor near the gas pedal. *You see?* he said to himself. He had had a feeling that was going to happen.

He decided the wrench needed sharpening again, and wearily he started fishing around on the floor. He spent the next hour grinding away at the edge, forcing himself to do five strokes at a time. Finally he had some sort of an edge on the tool.

This time he gave himself a pep talk. *You're going to do it right,* he told himself. *You're going to hold the chisel at just the right angle. Your hands will be sure and confident. And the chisel will make a cut. And then you'll do it again and make another cut. Watch me, Dad, I'm going to pretend I'm you. Then everything will work out just right.*

Forcing himself to concentrate, he got off a sharp, solid blow. The shock ran through his arm. *You see,* he told himself, *you've got marvelous hands. Now just concentrate and do the same thing again. Come on, sure shot, you can do it.* And he did, he got in seven or eight blows before the strength left his arm and he dropped the wrench. He lay back and closed his eyes.

Sometime later he woke up. Lightly he touched his right arm. He ought to take the bandage off and look at the wound, but it was too much trouble. Anyway, he didn't have time. He had to get back to work. He peered down as he placed the sharp end against the piece of metal. For a moment he was surprised at what he saw. He had actually managed to cut through half of the high point of the arch. The metal was twisting back in a jagged curl. He attacked the notch again, whacked the lug wrench with half a dozen solid blows. Then he stopped to resharpen the tool.

Slowly he ran the stone back and forth over the metal edge. He leaned forward to look at the metal trapping his foot. Yes, it was definitely being cut. He would close his eyes for just a moment. He would count slowly to one hundred, then go back to work.

Renewed after his short rest, he placed the chisel end against the notch and struck the tool. It bit in. Another half-dozen strikes and he checked the metal again. Unless his eyes were playing tricks on him, and maybe they were, the legs of the arch were definitely spreading. In fact, he might even — no, he had better not try, not yet. But he was getting there.

Leaning forward, he began hammering on the lug wrench. *Hands, don't fail me now*, he pleaded. This time, on the second blow, he felt a definite give in the metal. He pushed the lug wrench in and exerted pressure on one side. One leg of the arch gave way. He pried some more, then dropped the wrench and screamed, "I'm free! I'm out!"

Tears coursed down his cheeks. He was free!

He was going to live! He was going to see his home and family again!

Carefully he moved his foot to one side, then to the other. Holding his breath, he withdrew it slowly. For a moment the boot caught on the metal, then the leather scraped through, and he was able to move his whole leg, though not without pain. But if ever pain felt good, this was sheer pleasure.

He stuck his head through the window on the passenger's side and tried to push off, but his legs refused to work. Using his arms, he squirmed his way through the window until he tumbled outside and fell to the soggy ground. Lying on his stomach, he crawled forward to a patch of sunshine and passed out.

Half an hour later he came to and rolled over on his back to face the sky. How good the sun felt on his face, he thought. He would lie there for a while, drying out. He needed a rest before he tackled that cliff. It was a good hundred-foot climb to the road, and he wanted to get up there before dark. He didn't think he could survive another night without help of some kind. He figured it was around noon. He would rest until the sun reached the bottom of that big pine tree on the other side of the stream.

In half an hour his clothes were much drier, and he was able to sit up, take off his shirt, and look at his arm. To his surprise, the wound appeared clean, the opening much smaller than it had been. The flesh was wrinkled, but the infection had almost all disappeared. Certainly there was no sign of any pus. Perhaps being soaked in water had helped clear it up. He spread his bandage over a rock to dry.

Off to his right about ten feet away, Flash and Trigger appeared. "Well, the Great Klutz finally made it," he told them.

Rolling over on his stomach, Jimmy braced his arms up under his chest and tried to stand up. He got to his feet, stood upright for a few moments, then staggered forward and grabbed the trunk of a young pine just in time. He sank to his knees. His legs weren't used to bearing his weight. They were too weak. How could he ever climb on them?

He thought of the lug wrench in the car. He could dig the sharp end into the ground to steady himself and pull himself along. He turned around, crawled back to the car, and reached inside for the lug wrench. He looked around. Was there anything else he needed? The food was all gone. The keys? No one was going to drive off with the car. His eyes fell on the toolbox. Leaning through the window, he opened the lid and took out the section of broken rule. He slipped it into a back pocket of his Levi's and then retreated, taking the lug wrench with him.

Half-hopping, half-dragging one leg, he managed to wade across the stream without falling. Then, using the lug wrench to stab holds, he slowly and painfully made his way up the far bank, resting every few minutes. Once he was stopped by a ten-foot-high bench of rock and had to crawl on a narrow ledge for thirty feet before he found a gully that would let him continue upward. Halfway to the top he found his camera, seemingly none the worse for wear. He looped the strap around his neck and continued to climb.

Several times he passed out for short periods, lying on narrow ledges, his legs jammed against the young trees that had gained a foothold here and there on the steep slope. Once he dropped the lug wrench, and it clattered down six feet or so and lodged in some bushes. He was now within forty feet of the road, and he was tempted to leave it there but feared he would need it again. Wearily he turned back, retreated to the clump of bushes, picked up the wrench, and grimly resumed his efforts.

It seemed to take all afternoon, but finally he was within ten feet of the road — and he heard a car coming! He shouted to the driver, but the man did not hear him and did not stop. Jimmy sank down between two rocks. *Get going*, he told himself. The last few feet were sheer hell. He was deathly afraid of losing his grip and tumbling all the way to the bottom. But finally he dragged his body up over the edge and lay full-length on the gravel at the side of the road.

For a good hour he lay in the sunlight, resting and dozing. Then he decided he ought to stand up so as to be more visible. He dragged himself to his feet and tottered down to where a large ponderosa pine grew beside the road. He leaned against the rough bark of the tree and waited. Surely it wouldn't be long now?

He found that he couldn't stay on his feet. Slowly he slid down the bark until he was sitting on his haunches. He reached out and began to pluck and eat handfuls of coarse grass. He must have eaten a bowlful of the weed before his stomach rebelled and he began to throw up.

He was on all fours, heaving his guts out, when he heard the truck in the distance. He sat up against the tree and waited. Soon an empty logging truck came around a curve and into view. The vehicle slowed down, stopped, and the driver climbed out.

"What's wrong?" he asked, coming over to Jimmy.

"I was in a wreck," Jimmy said. "My car's down there." He pointed into the ravine.

"Can you stand up?" the driver asked. "Do you have any broken bones?"

Jimmy shook his head. "Just some cuts, is all."

"Anyone else down there?" the driver asked.

"I'm all alone," Jimmy said.

The driver placed Jimmy's arm around his shoulders.

"My wrench," Jimmy said. "I need that wrench."

The driver picked up the wrench, then assisted Jimmy to the truck. He had to lift him up and push him into the cab. Then he swung in on the opposite side. "When did it happen?" he asked, shifting into low gear and releasing the brake.

"It happened . . ." Jimmy said. "Wait a minute. What's today's date?"

"Saturday," the driver said.

"Saturday? July twelfth?"

"Yes."

"Tomorrow's my birthday," Jimmy said with a weak grin.

"Well, hey, this is no way to celebrate your birthday," the driver replied. "I mean, wrecking your car like that."

"Two weeks ago," Jimmy said. "I went into the ravine almost two weeks ago." He turned his head to look back at the spot where he had run off the road. In his mind's eye the deer took off again from the side of the road, launching its body upward. Then a wave of blackness swept over Jimmy, and he fell sideways on the seat.

The driver swore, grabbed the handmike, and flipped the switch. "Breaker, breaker, this is Fast Frenchy. I need medical assistance. I need Smokey or an ambulance. Who's out there? Breaker, breaker, this is Fast Frenchy."

Chapter Sixteen

The next evening everyone was crowded around Jimmy's bed in the county hospital: his mother, his dad, Andy, and Candy.

"Are you ready to come home?" his mother asked. "We have a big birthday party planned for tomorrow. It's a day late, but better late than never."

"You better believe I'm ready to come," Jimmy said. Then he added with a grin, "Hey, I sure missed you guys!"

"We missed you," his mother said. "Your dad didn't get more than two hours of sleep a night since you disappeared. He's been driving up and down the roads like a wild man."

"I climbed down there yesterday, son," his father said, "to see where you were. I still don't believe it. I just don't know how you managed to cut yourself free."

Jimmy reached under the bed and dragged out the lug wrench. The truck driver had left it and the camera with him the previous evening, when he brought Jimmy into the hospital.

"With that, Dad." Jimmy handed over the wrench. "I sharpened one end into a chisel and hit the other end with a rock until I cut through the piece of metal that was trapping my foot."

His father turned the tool over in his hands, carefully examining the chisel end. "I still don't see how you did it. I mean, how did you get an edge on this thing?"

Jimmy explained how he had managed the whole process. Then he told them about the two chipmunks, and his signals and breathing tube, and the flood that had almost drowned him.

His father shook his head. "I still can't get over it. You know what the sheriff said when he saw the car? 'This guy made Houdini look like an amateur.'"

Jimmy grinned. "And I was always clumsy with tools, right, Dad?"

"How come you've kept your talents hidden all these years?" his father asked.

"Aw, Dad, I didn't want to cut in on your turf." Jimmy turned to his mother and asked, "What did the doctors tell you, Mom?"

"You're to get lots of rest for the next few days. And we're to feed you plenty."

"I lost thirty pounds," Jimmy said. "When they weighed me I was down to one hundred and twenty."

"How's the arm feel?" his mother asked.

"Fine. They didn't even have to put stitches in it."

"And your leg?" his dad asked.

"Still a bit weak," Jimmy said. "But they're

giving me a program of exercises to do when I get home. They say there's no reason I won't get back full use of that foot."

"I'd say you were one very lucky young man," his mother said.

"One very *plucky* young man," his father corrected.

"He's a hero, and as soon as we get home, I'm going to bake him a big batch of chocolate-chip cookies," Candy said.

"Hey, Jimmy," Andy said. "I went down there and took pictures of the car. Will you autograph them for me?"

"Sure, but why?"

"I'm going to sell them for two bucks apiece," Andy explained. "I already got orders for six pictures."

"Hey, wait a minute," Jimmy protested. "You got to cut me in. I want at least one dollar per photo."

Andy's face fell. "Aw, then it's not worth it. I have to pay for the film, and developing, and . . ."

Jimmy grinned. "Forget it. I was only kidding."

"You heard about Charlene?" his mother asked.

"Don't tell me, let me guess," Jimmy said. "Wayne came home on leave, and they got married by Judge Twitchell, and then they took off for San Francisco on their honeymoon."

"I see someone has already called you from home with all the news," his mother said.

"No, Mom," Jimmy said with a grin. "I just had a lot of time down there to figure things out."

"What's this?" His dad picked up the broken rule from the bedside table.

"Just something I found in the wagon," Jimmy said.

He didn't want to tell his dad what that rule meant to him, that he would always keep it to remind himself of his ordeal, of his realization that nobody could tell him what he was good at or bad at, that from now on only Jimmy Korne was responsible for what Jimmy Korne could or could no tdo. And Jimmy Korne had said goodbye to the Great Klutz down in the ravine.

"It's a long story, Dad," Jimmy finally said. "Someday I'll tell you."